w   w
9.13 10.16

DE   12

MORE PRAISE FOR BABYMOUSE!

"Sassy, smart . . .
Babymouse is here
to stay."
—The Horn Book Magazine

"Young readers
will happily
fall in line."
—Kirkus Reviews

"The brother-sister creative team hits the mark
with humor, sweetness, and characters so genuine
they can pass for real kids." —Booklist

"Babymouse is spunky, ambitious,
and, at times, a total dweeb."
—School Library Journal

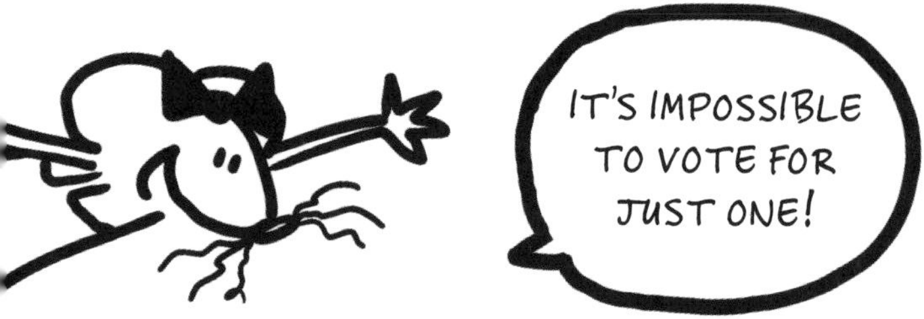
IT'S IMPOSSIBLE TO VOTE FOR JUST ONE!

BE SURE TO READ **ALL** THE **BABYMOUSE** BOOKS:

#1 BABYMOUSE: Queen of the World!
#2 BABYMOUSE: Our Hero
#3 BABYMOUSE: Beach Babe
#4 BABYMOUSE: Rock Star
#5 BABYMOUSE: Heartbreaker
#6 CAMP BABYMOUSE
#7 BABYMOUSE: Skater Girl
#8 BABYMOUSE: Puppy Love
#9 BABYMOUSE: Monster Mash
#10 BABYMOUSE: The Musical
#11 BABYMOUSE: Dragonslayer
#12 BABYMOUSE: Burns Rubber
#13 BABYMOUSE: Cupcake Tycoon
#14 BABYMOUSE: Mad Scientist
#15 A Very BABYMOUSE Christmas
#16 BABYMOUSE for President

BABYMOUSE

FOR PRESIDENT

SEAL OF THE PRESIDENT OF THE UNITED STATES OF CUPCAKES

BY JENNIFER L. HOLM & MATTHEW HOLM

RANDOM HOUSE 🏠 NEW YORK

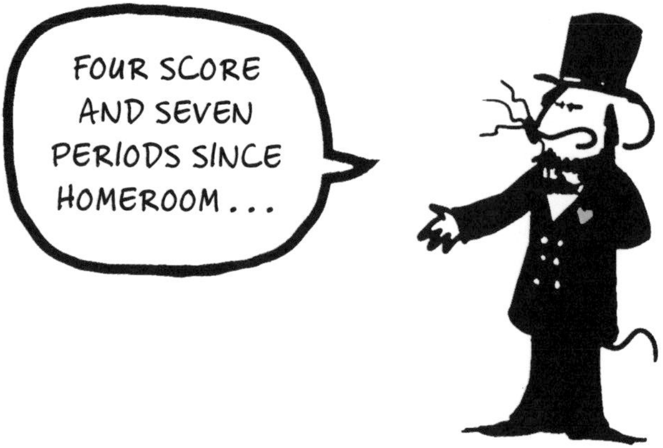
FOUR SCORE AND SEVEN PERIODS SINCE HOMEROOM . . .

This is a work of fiction. Names, characters, places, and incidents either are the product of the authors' imagination or are used fictitiously. Any resemblance to actual persons, living or dead, events, or locales is entirely coincidental.

Published in the United States by Random House Children's Books, a division of Random House, Inc., New York.

Random House and the colophon are registered trademarks of Random House, Inc.

Visit us on the Web! randomhouse.com/kids

Educators and librarians, for a variety of teaching tools, visit us at randomhouse.com/teachers

Babymouse.com

Library of Congress Cataloging-in-Publication Data
Babymouse for president / by Jennifer L. Holm and Matthew Holm. — 1st ed.
p. cm.
Summary: When Babymouse decides to become president of the student council, she learns that there is more to running for office than being famous and in charge.
ISBN 978-0-375-86780-4 (trade pbk.) — ISBN 978-0-375-96780-1 (lib. bdg.)
1. Graphic novels. [1. Graphic novels. 2. Politics, Practical—Fiction. 3. Schools—Fiction. 4. Mice—Fiction.] I. Holm, Matthew. II. Title.
PZ7.7.H65Baff 2012 741.5'973—dc23 2011024118

MANUFACTURED IN MALAYSIA
10 9 8 7 6 5 4 3 2 1
First Edition

Random House Children's Books supports the First Amendment and celebrates the right to read.

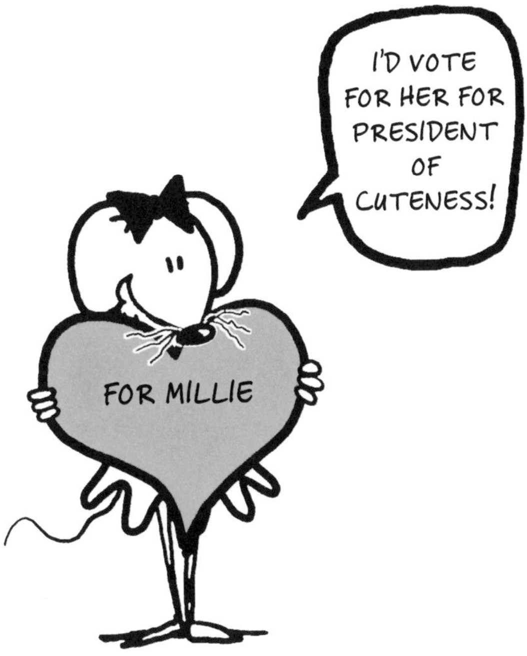
FOR MILLIE
I'D VOTE FOR HER FOR PRESIDENT OF CUTENESS!

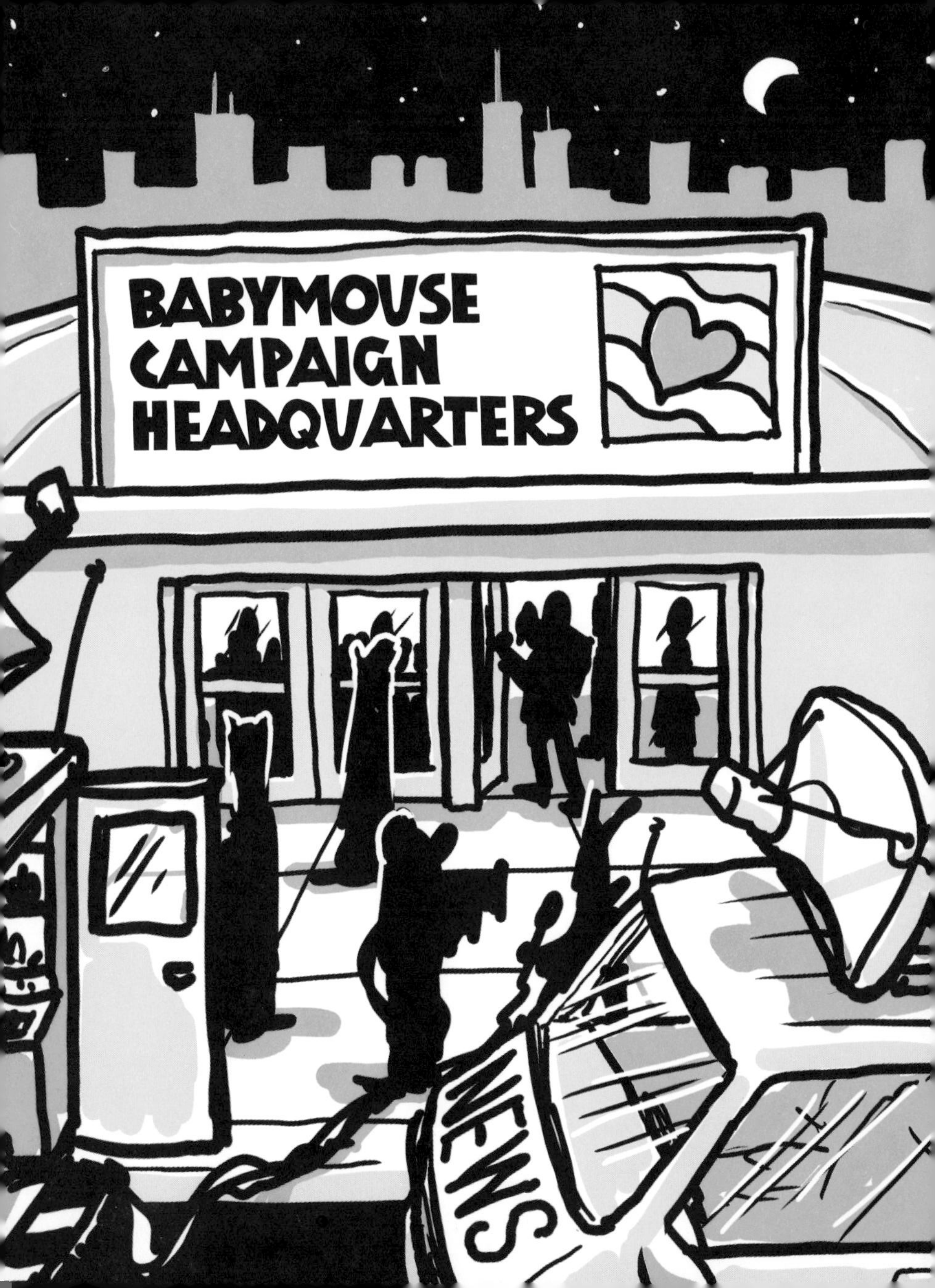
BABYMOUSE
CAMPAIGN
HEADQUARTERS
NEWS

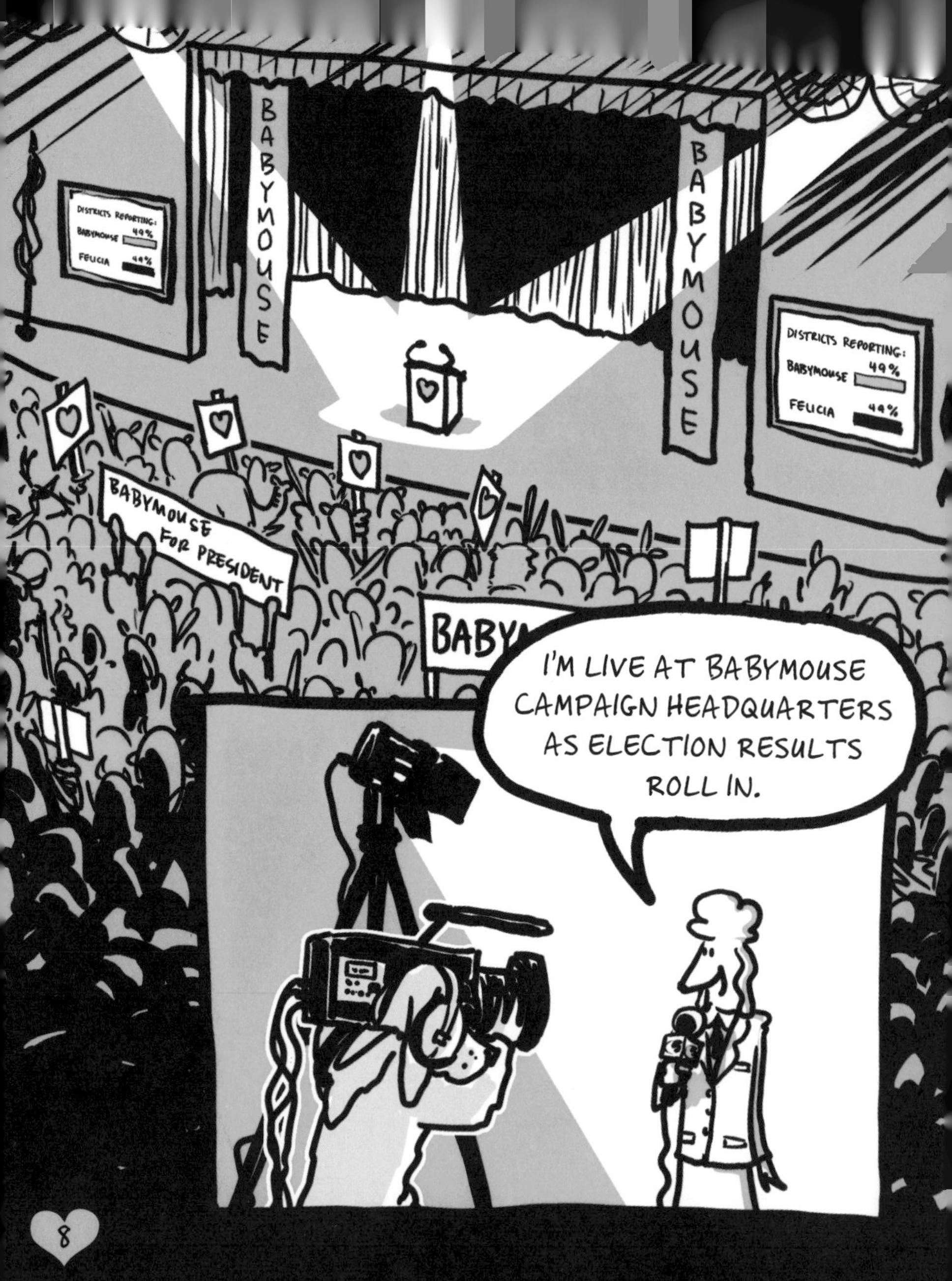
DISTRICTS REPORTING:
BABYMOUSE 49%
FELICIA 49%
BABYMOUSE
BABYMOUSE
DISTRICTS REPORTING:
BABYMOUSE 49%
FELICIA 49%
BABYMOUSE FOR PRESIDENT
I'M LIVE AT BABYMOUSE CAMPAIGN HEADQUARTERS AS ELECTION RESULTS ROLL IN.

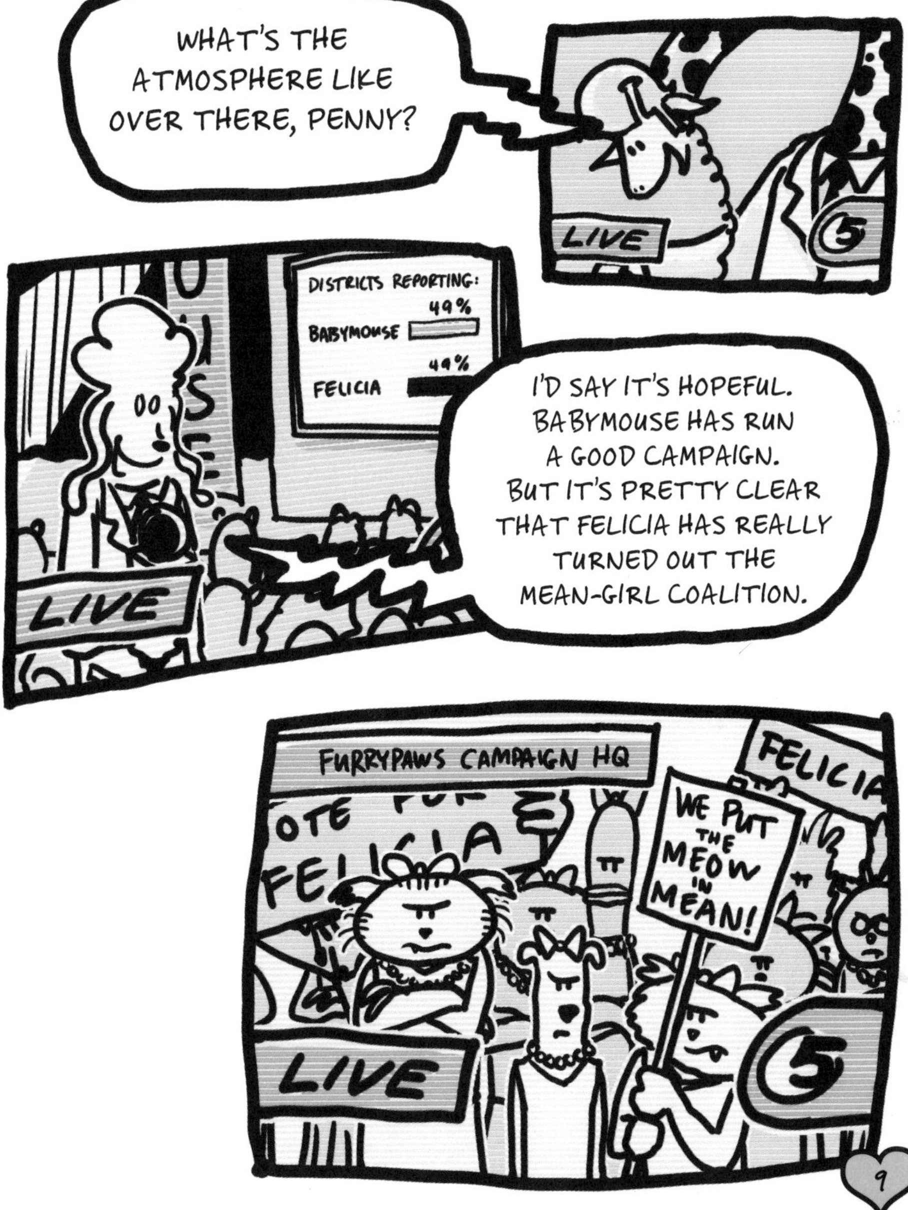
WHAT'S THE ATMOSPHERE LIKE OVER THERE, PENNY?
LIVE
5
DISTRICTS REPORTING:
49%
BABYMOUSE
49%
FELICIA
LIVE
I'D SAY IT'S HOPEFUL. BABYMOUSE HAS RUN A GOOD CAMPAIGN. BUT IT'S PRETTY CLEAR THAT FELICIA HAS REALLY TURNED OUT THE MEAN-GIRL COALITION.
FURRYPAWS CAMPAIGN HQ
FELICIA
WE PUT THE MEOW IN MEAN!
LIVE
5

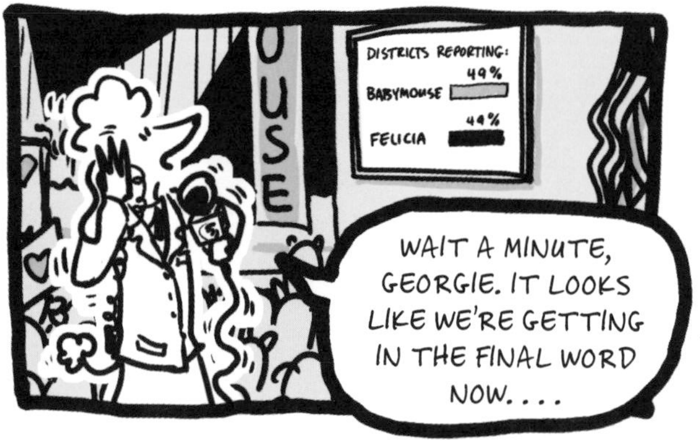
DISTRICTS REPORTING:
49%
BABYMOUSE
49%
FELICIA
WAIT A MINUTE, GEORGIE. IT LOOKS LIKE WE'RE GETTING IN THE FINAL WORD NOW. . . .

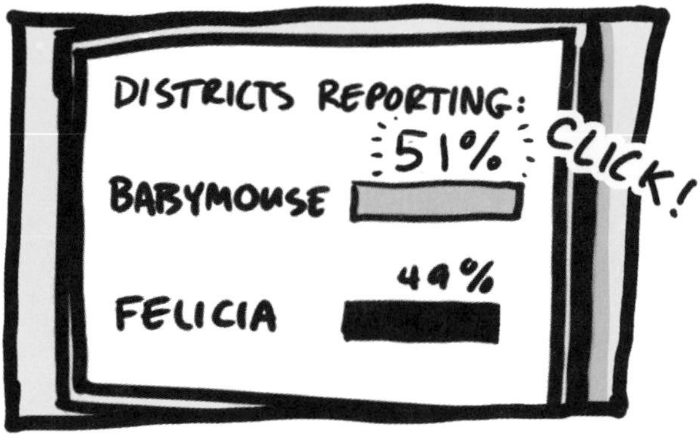
DISTRICTS REPORTING:
51%
BABYMOUSE
49%
FELICIA
CLICK!

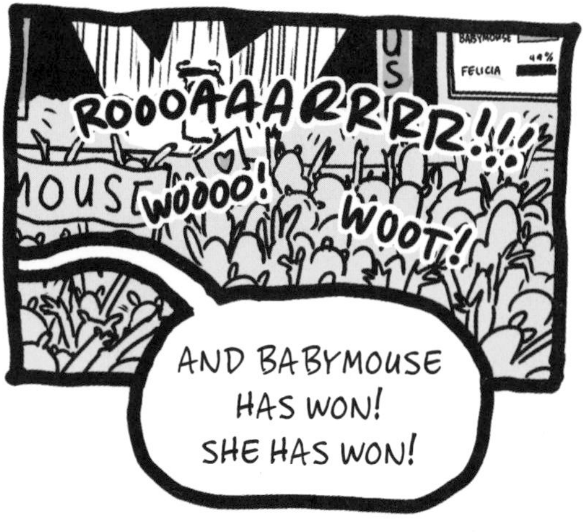
ROOOAAARRRR!!!
WOOOO!
WOOT!
AND BABYMOUSE HAS WON! SHE HAS WON!

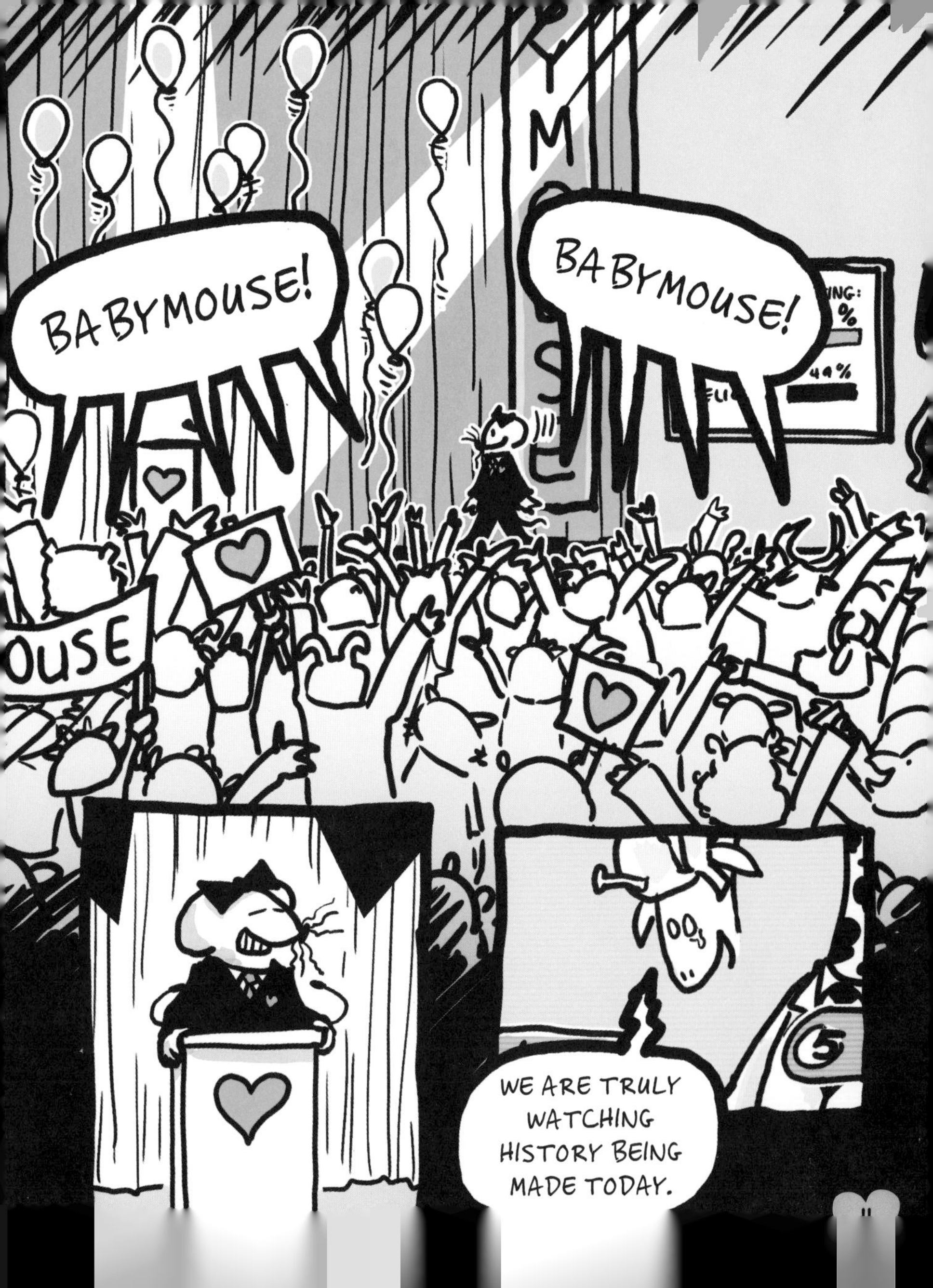
BABYMOUSE!
BABYMOUSE!
OUSE
WE ARE TRULY WATCHING HISTORY BEING MADE TODAY.

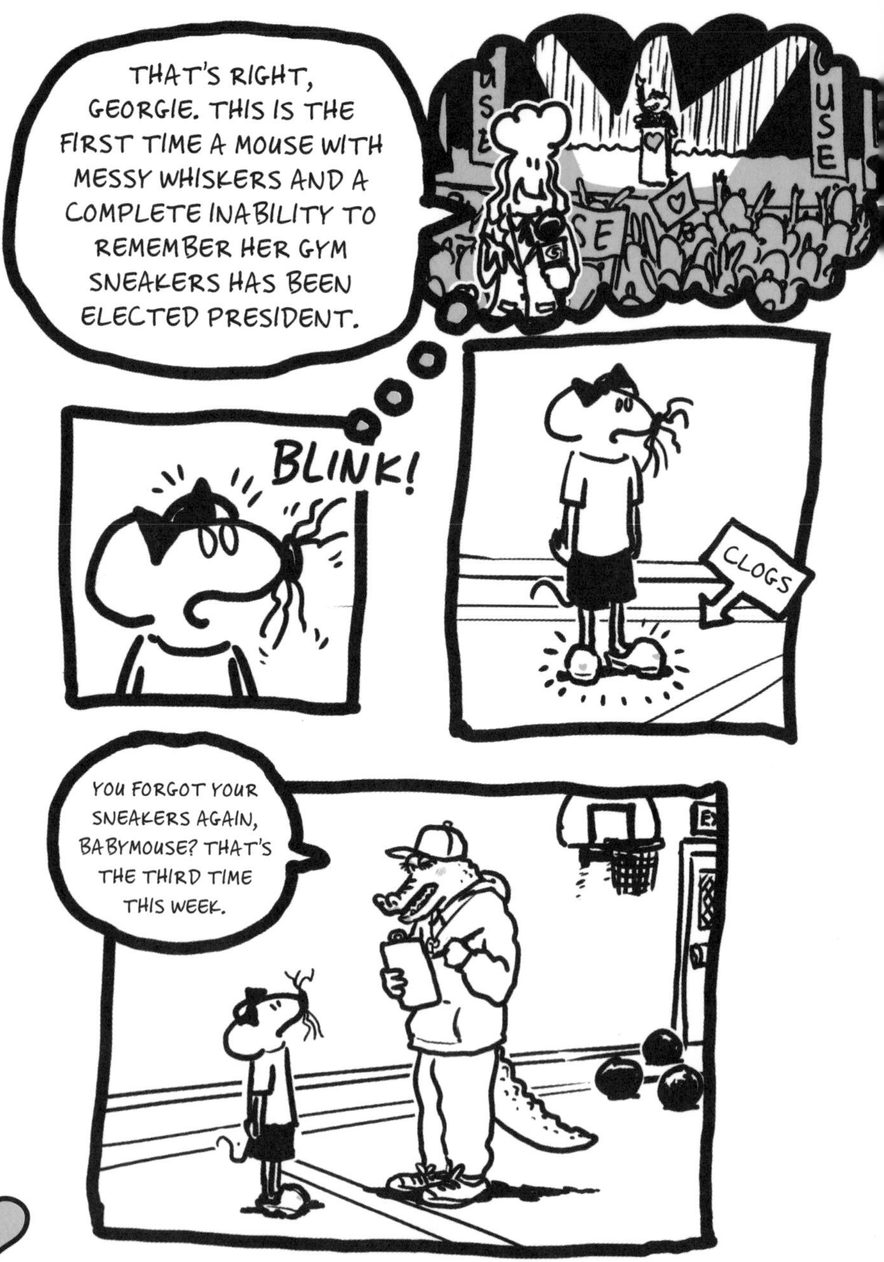
THAT'S RIGHT, GEORGIE. THIS IS THE FIRST TIME A MOUSE WITH MESSY WHISKERS AND A COMPLETE INABILITY TO REMEMBER HER GYM SNEAKERS HAS BEEN ELECTED PRESIDENT.
BLINK!
CLOGS
YOU FORGOT YOUR SNEAKERS AGAIN, BABYMOUSE? THAT'S THE THIRD TIME THIS WEEK.

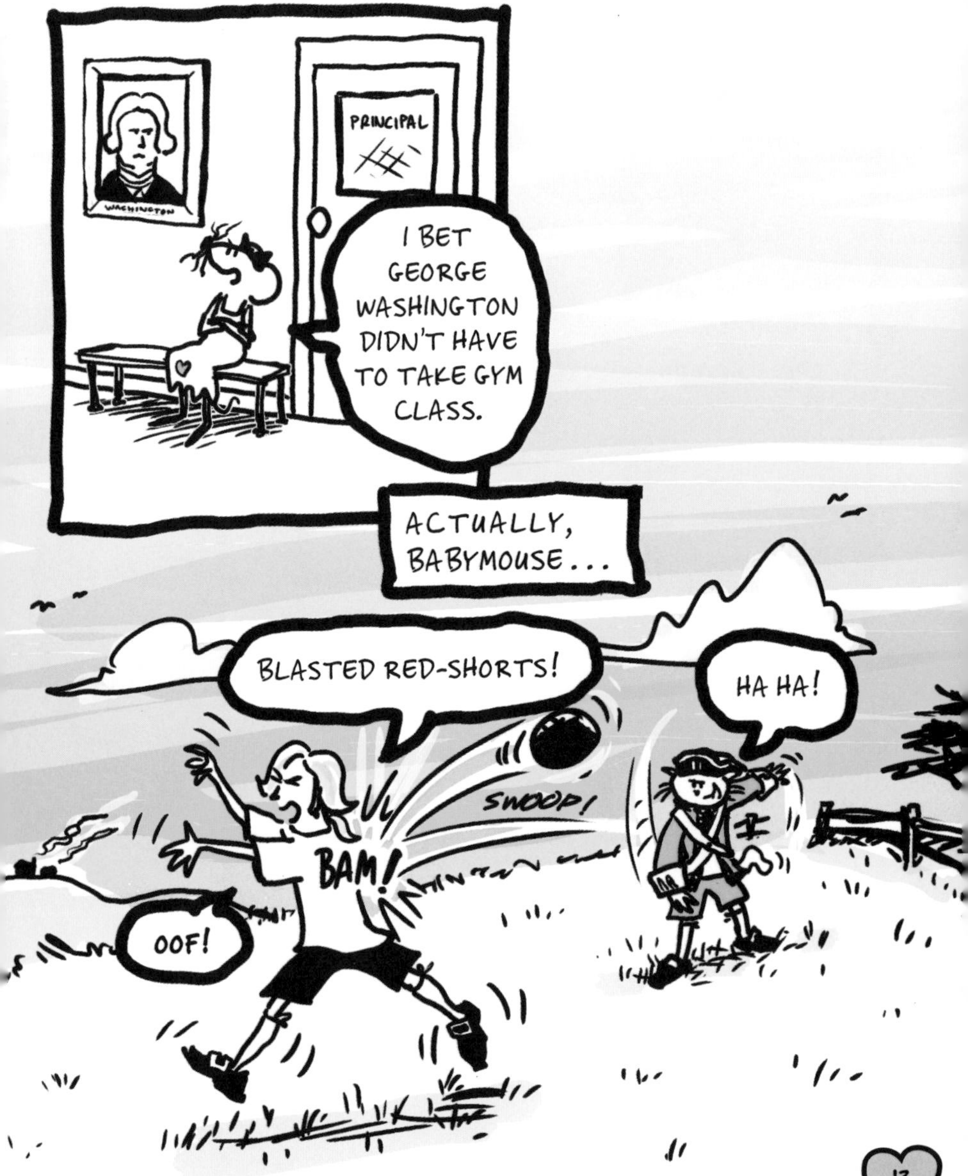
PRINCIPAL
WASHINGTON
I BET GEORGE WASHINGTON DIDN'T HAVE TO TAKE GYM CLASS.
ACTUALLY, BABYMOUSE...
BLASTED RED-SHORTS!
HA HA!
SWOOP!
BAM!
OOF!

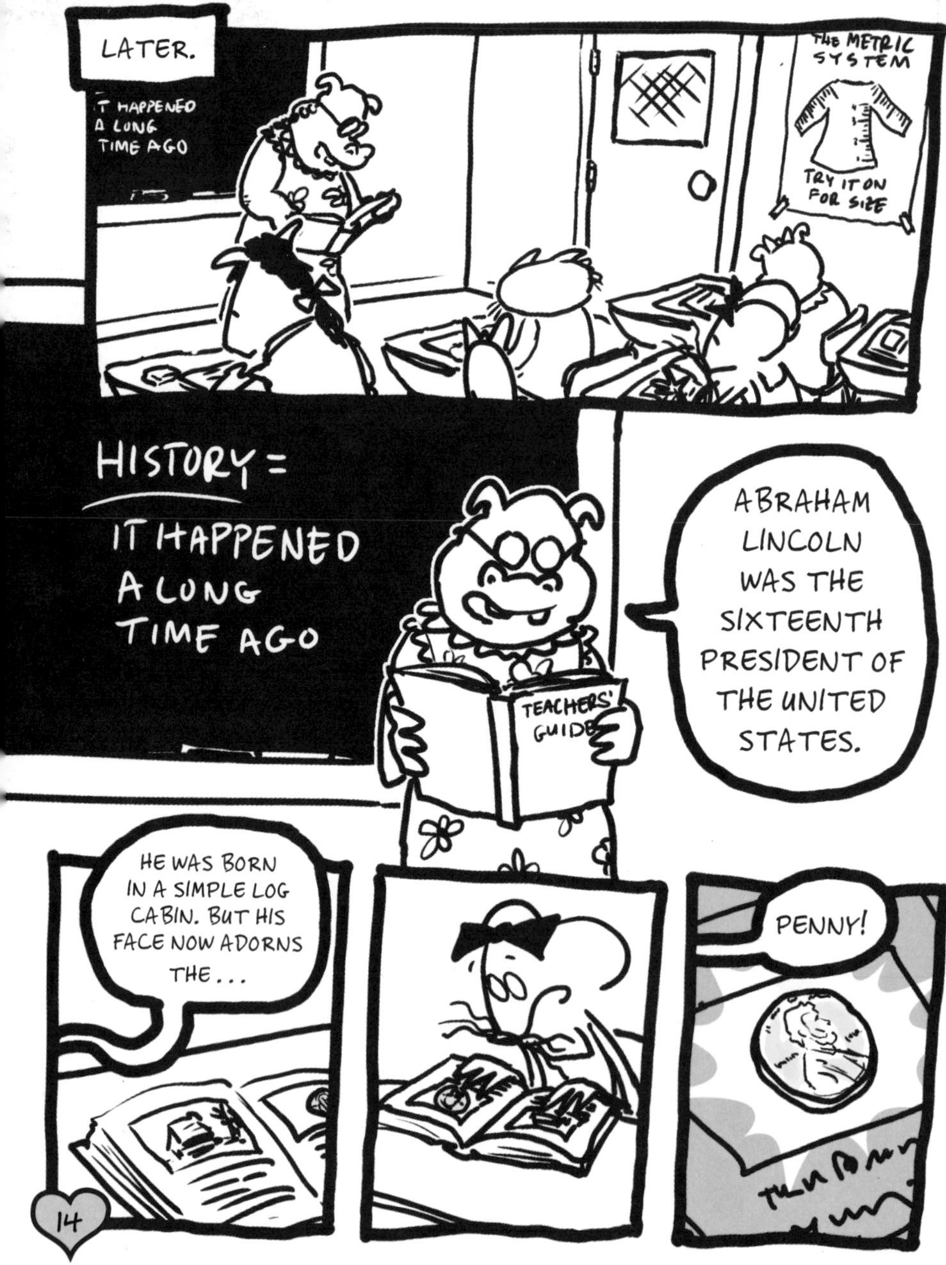
LATER.
IT HAPPENED A LONG TIME AGO
THE METRIC SYSTEM
TRY IT ON FOR SIZE
HISTORY =
IT HAPPENED A LONG TIME AGO
ABRAHAM LINCOLN WAS THE SIXTEENTH PRESIDENT OF THE UNITED STATES.
TEACHERS' GUIDE
HE WAS BORN IN A SIMPLE LOG CABIN. BUT HIS FACE NOW ADORNS THE...
PENNY!

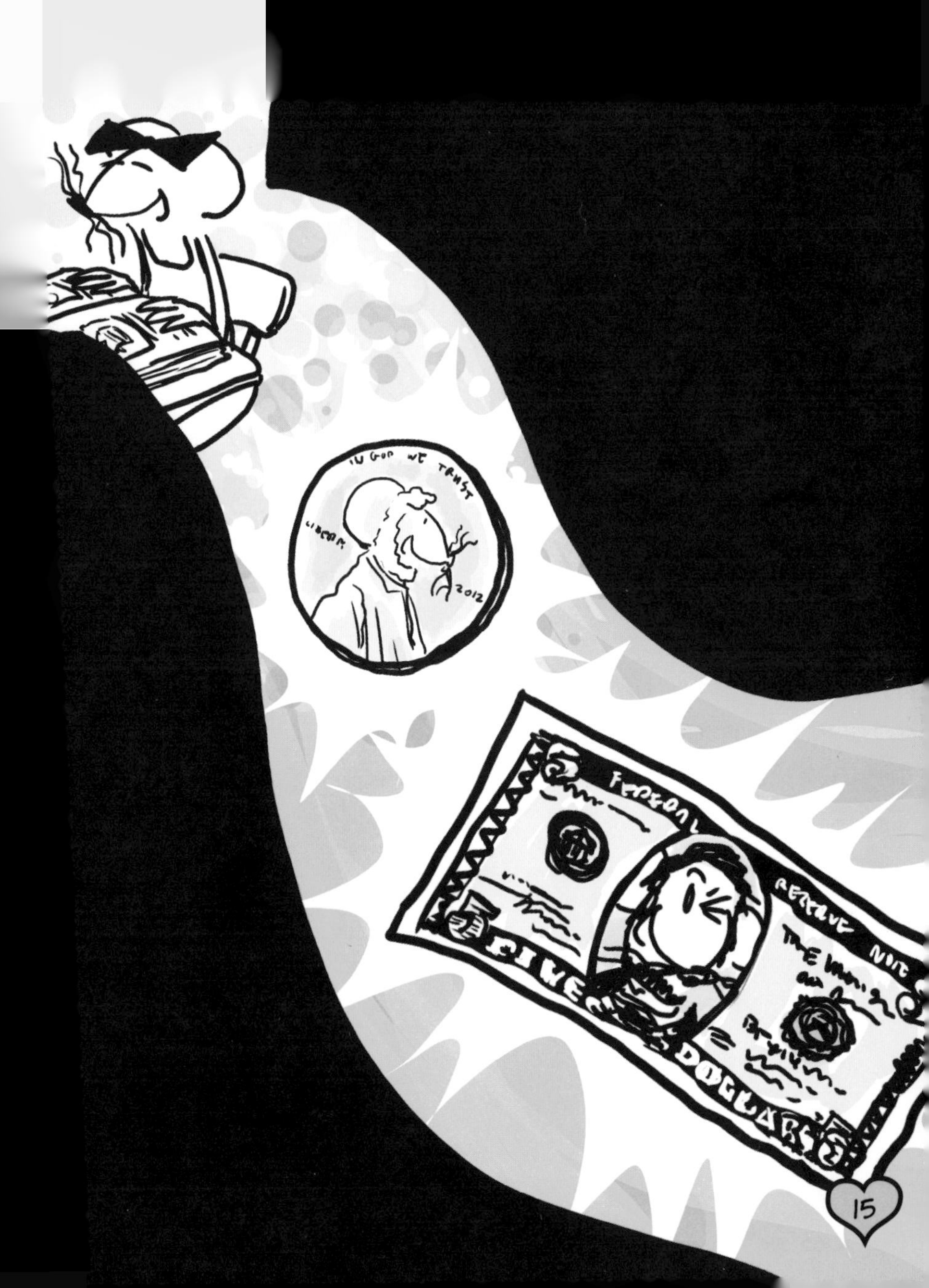
IN GOD WE TRUST
2012
FIVE
DOLLARS

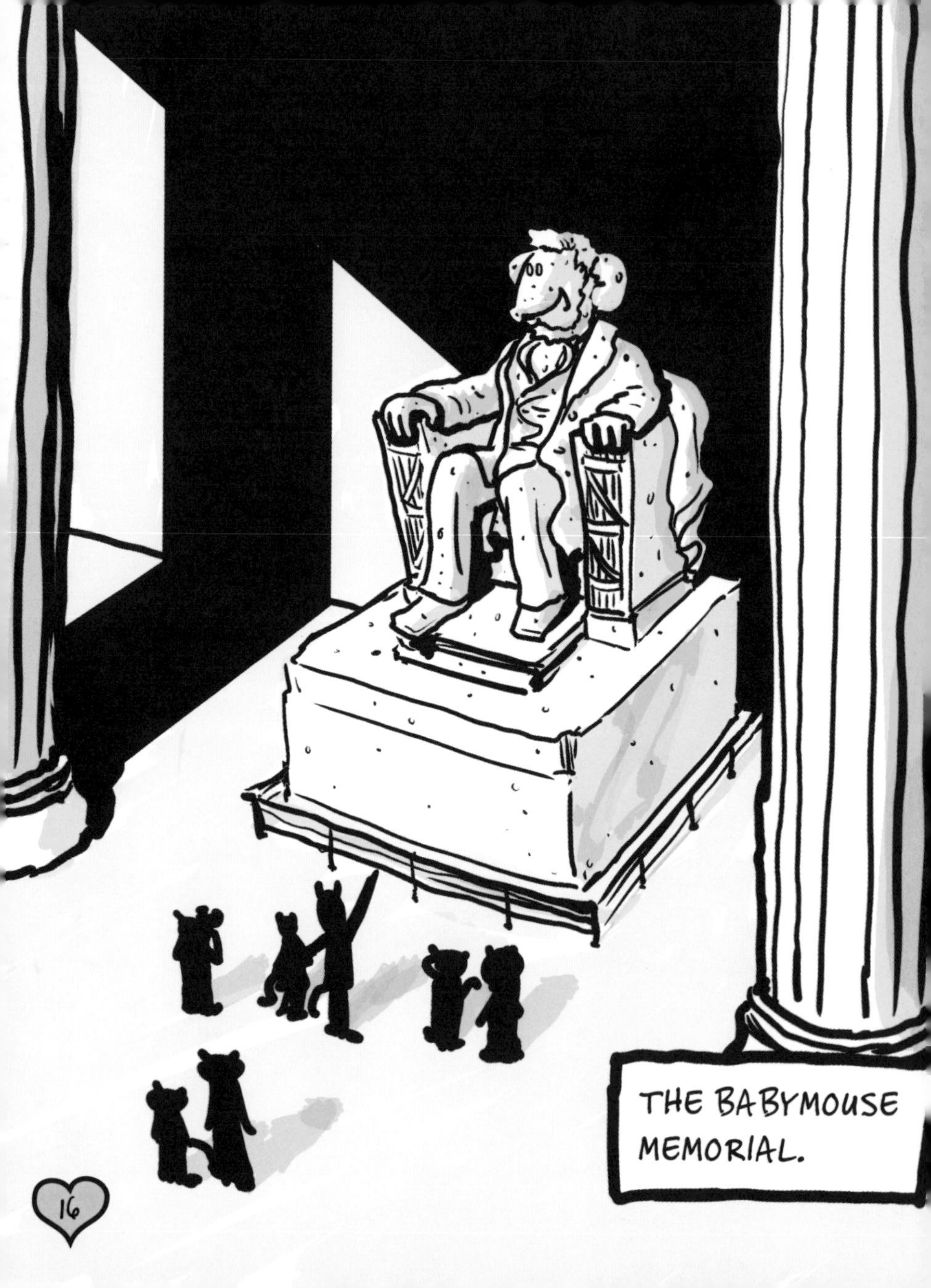
THE BABYMOUSE MEMORIAL.

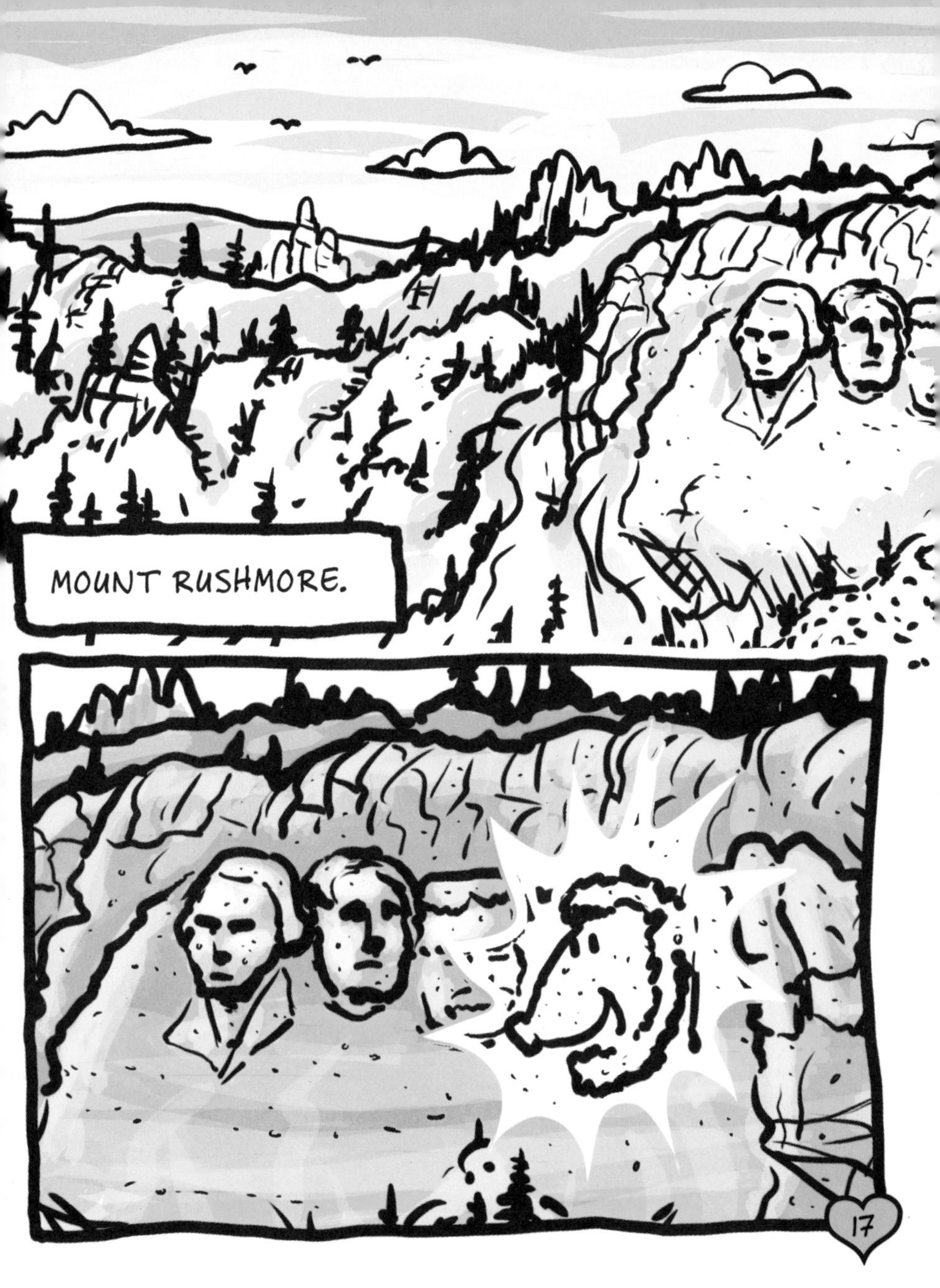
MOUNT RUSHMORE.

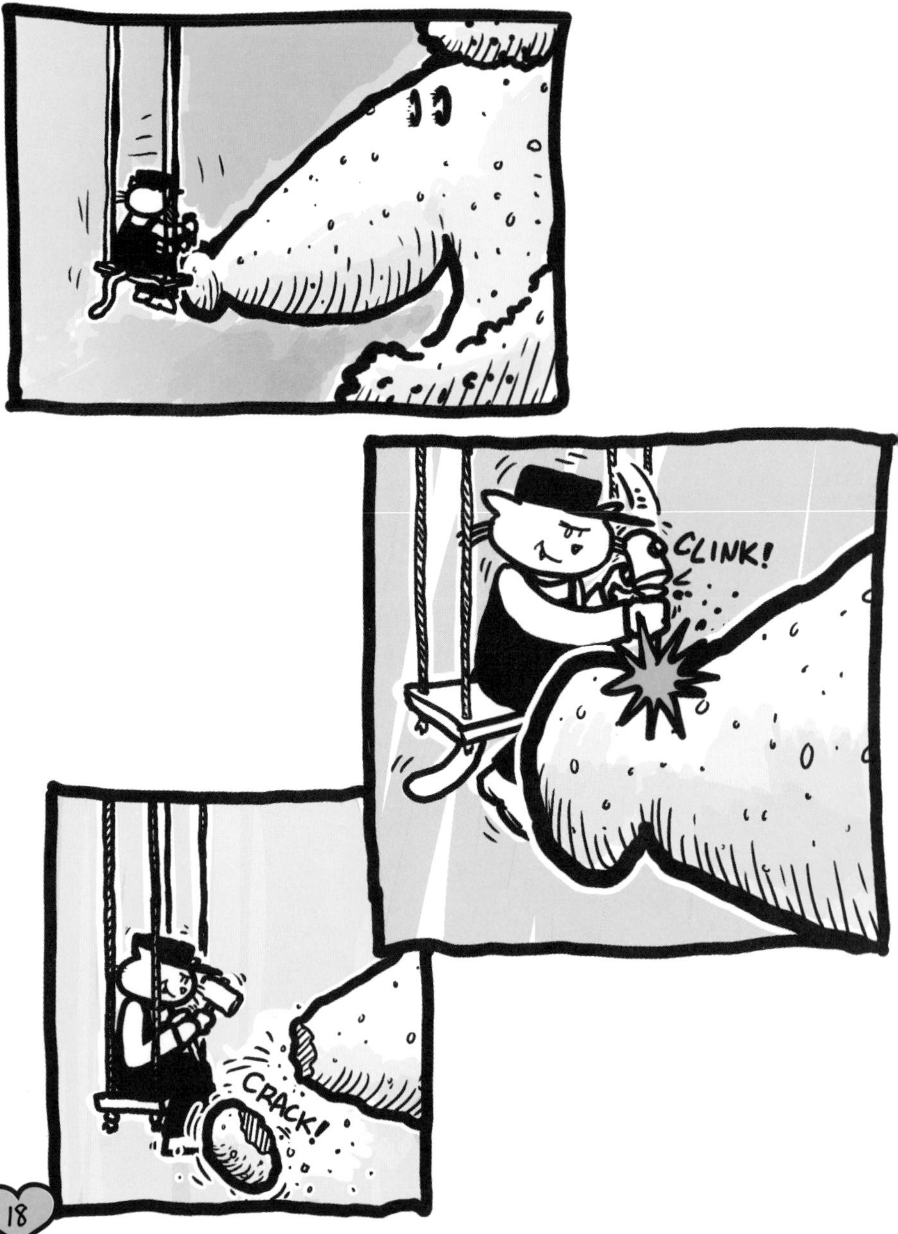
CLINK!
CRACK!

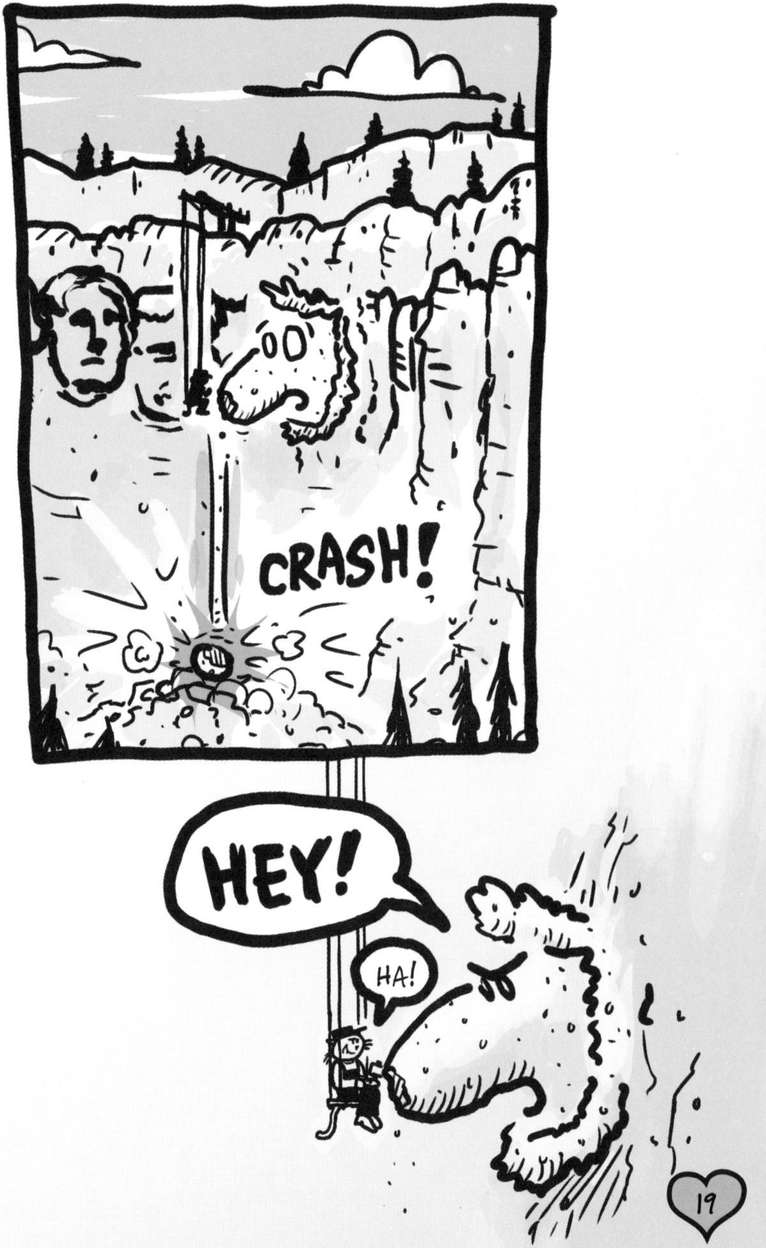
CRASH!
HEY!
HA!

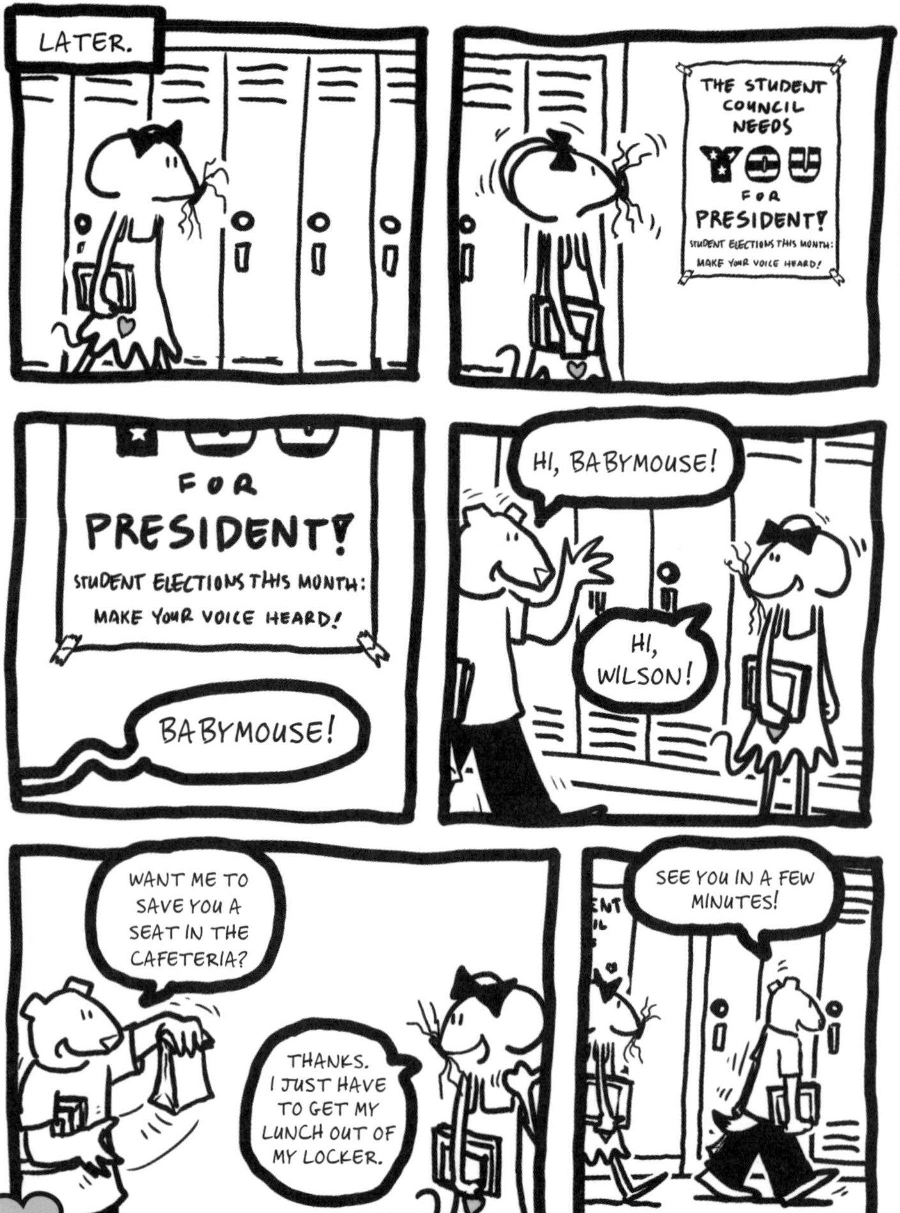
LATER.
THE STUDENT COUNCIL NEEDS YOU FOR PRESIDENT!
STUDENT ELECTIONS THIS MONTH:
MAKE YOUR VOICE HEARD!
FOR PRESIDENT!
STUDENT ELECTIONS THIS MONTH:
MAKE YOUR VOICE HEARD!
BABYMOUSE!
HI, BABYMOUSE!
HI, WILSON!
WANT ME TO SAVE YOU A SEAT IN THE CAFETERIA?
THANKS. I JUST HAVE TO GET MY LUNCH OUT OF MY LOCKER.
SEE YOU IN A FEW MINUTES!

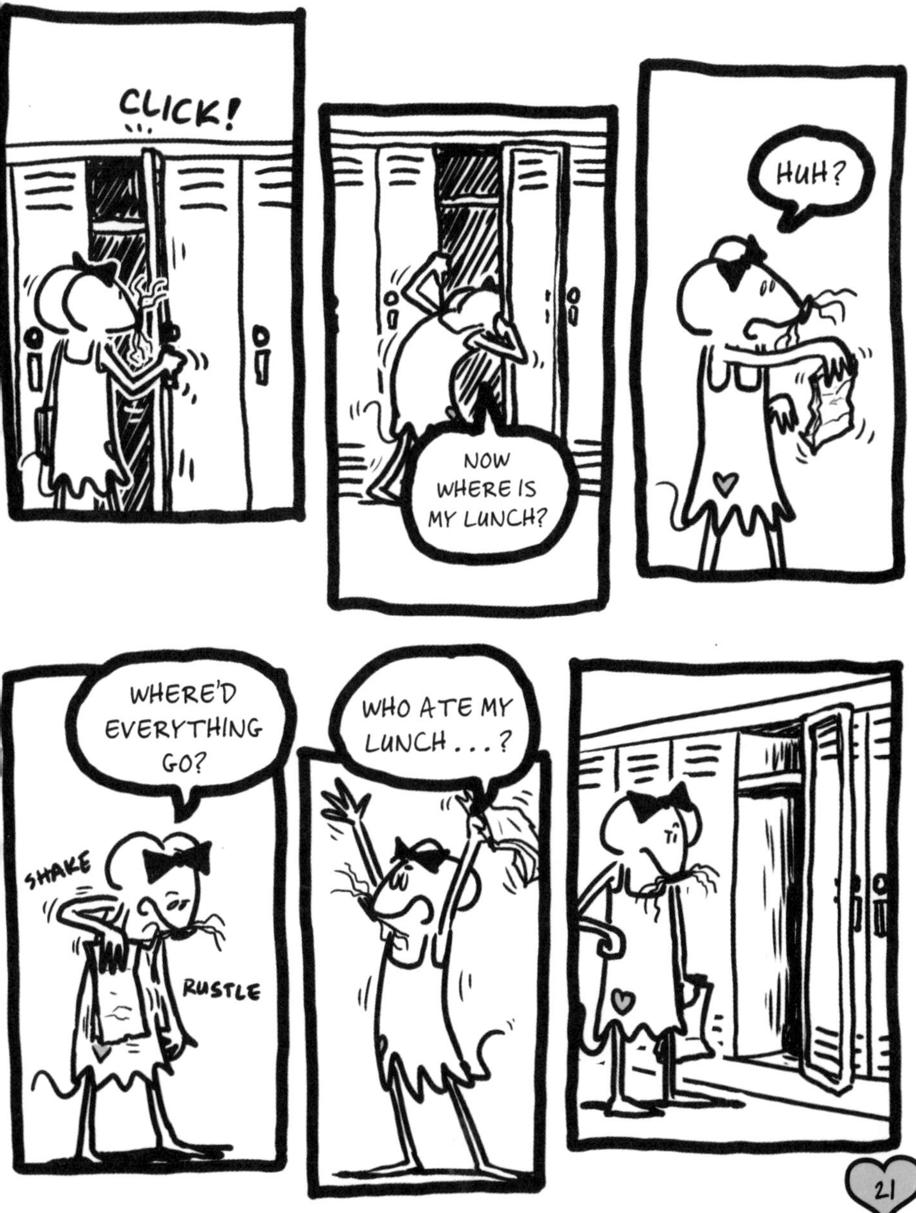
CLICK!
NOW WHERE IS MY LUNCH?
HUH?
WHERE'D EVERYTHING GO?
SHAKE
RUSTLE
WHO ATE MY LUNCH . . . ?

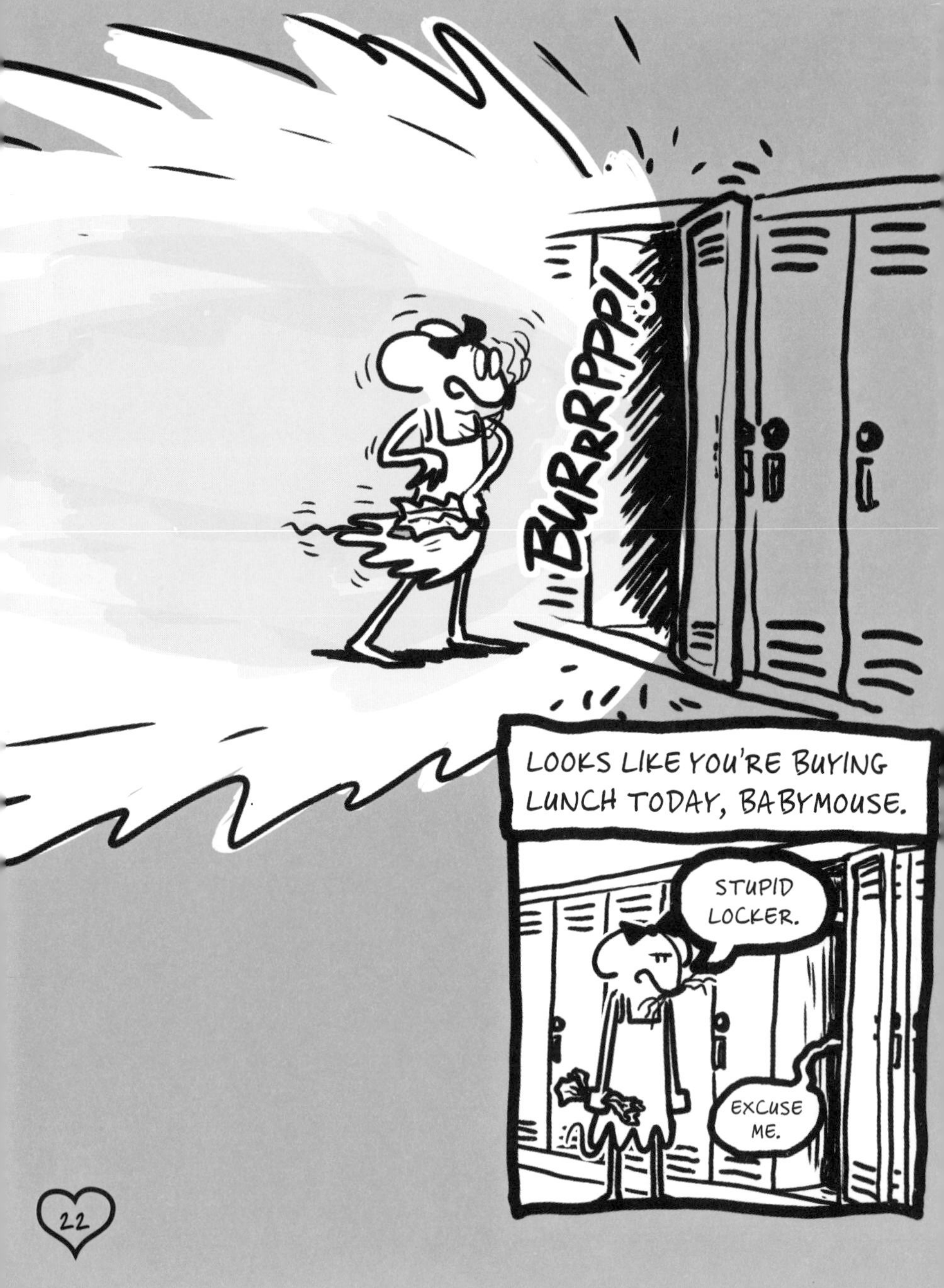
BURRRPPP!
LOOKS LIKE YOU'RE BUYING LUNCH TODAY, BABYMOUSE.
STUPID LOCKER.
EXCUSE ME.

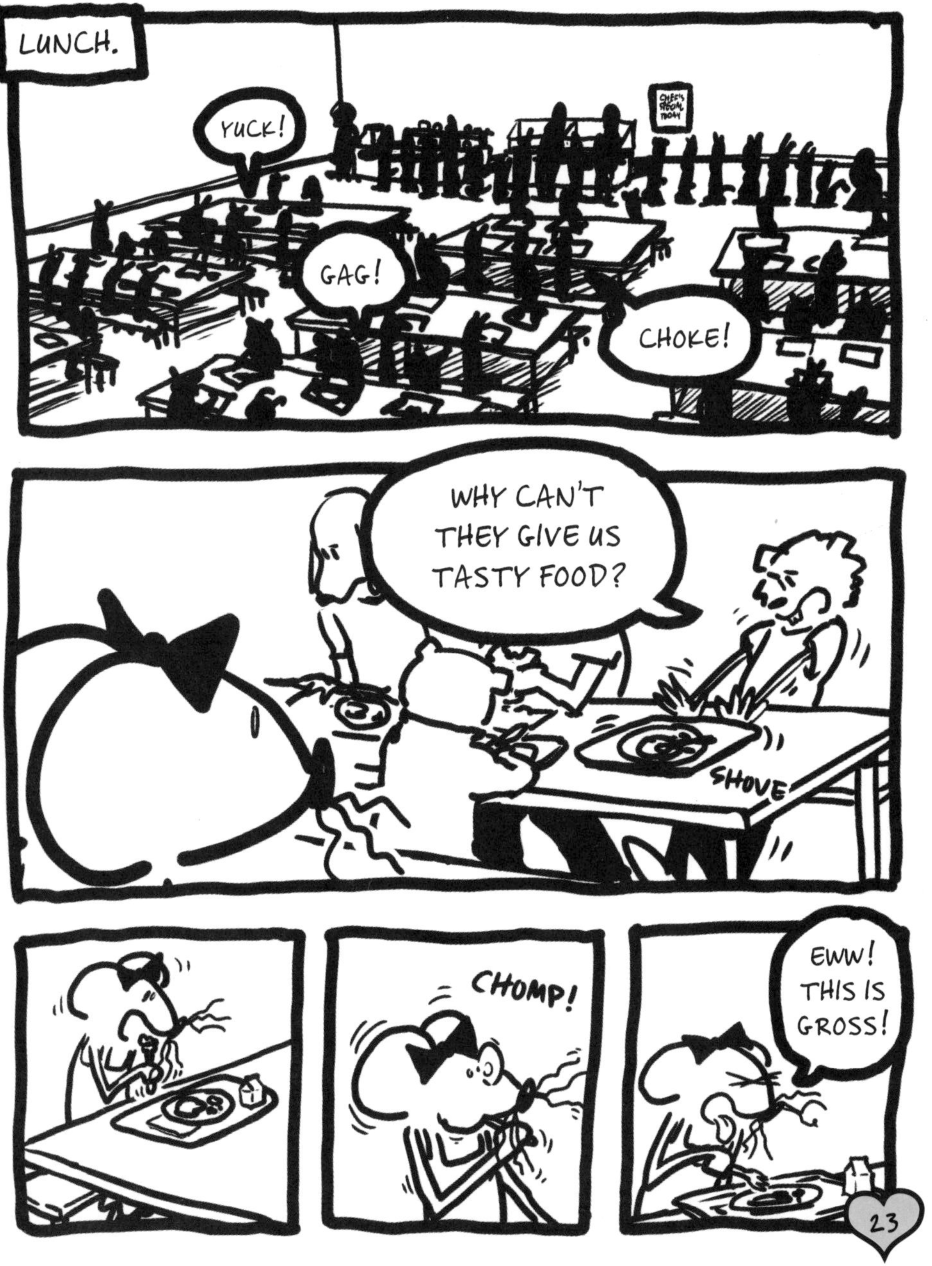
LUNCH.
YUCK!
GAG!
CHOKE!
WHY CAN'T THEY GIVE US TASTY FOOD?
SHOVE
CHOMP!
EWW! THIS IS GROSS!

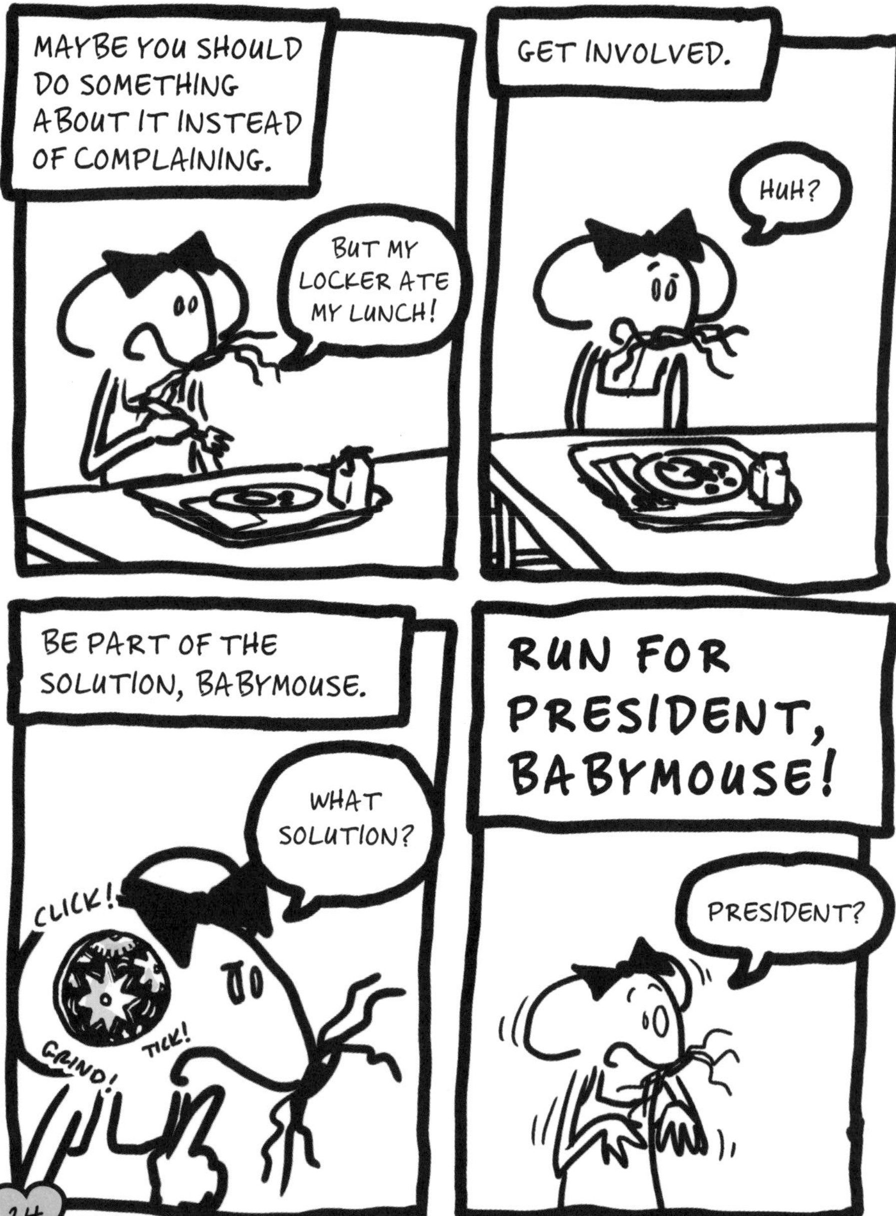
MAYBE YOU SHOULD DO SOMETHING ABOUT IT INSTEAD OF COMPLAINING.
BUT MY LOCKER ATE MY LUNCH!
GET INVOLVED.
HUH?
BE PART OF THE SOLUTION, BABYMOUSE.
WHAT SOLUTION?
CLICK!
TICK!
GRIND!
RUN FOR PRESIDENT, BABYMOUSE!
PRESIDENT?

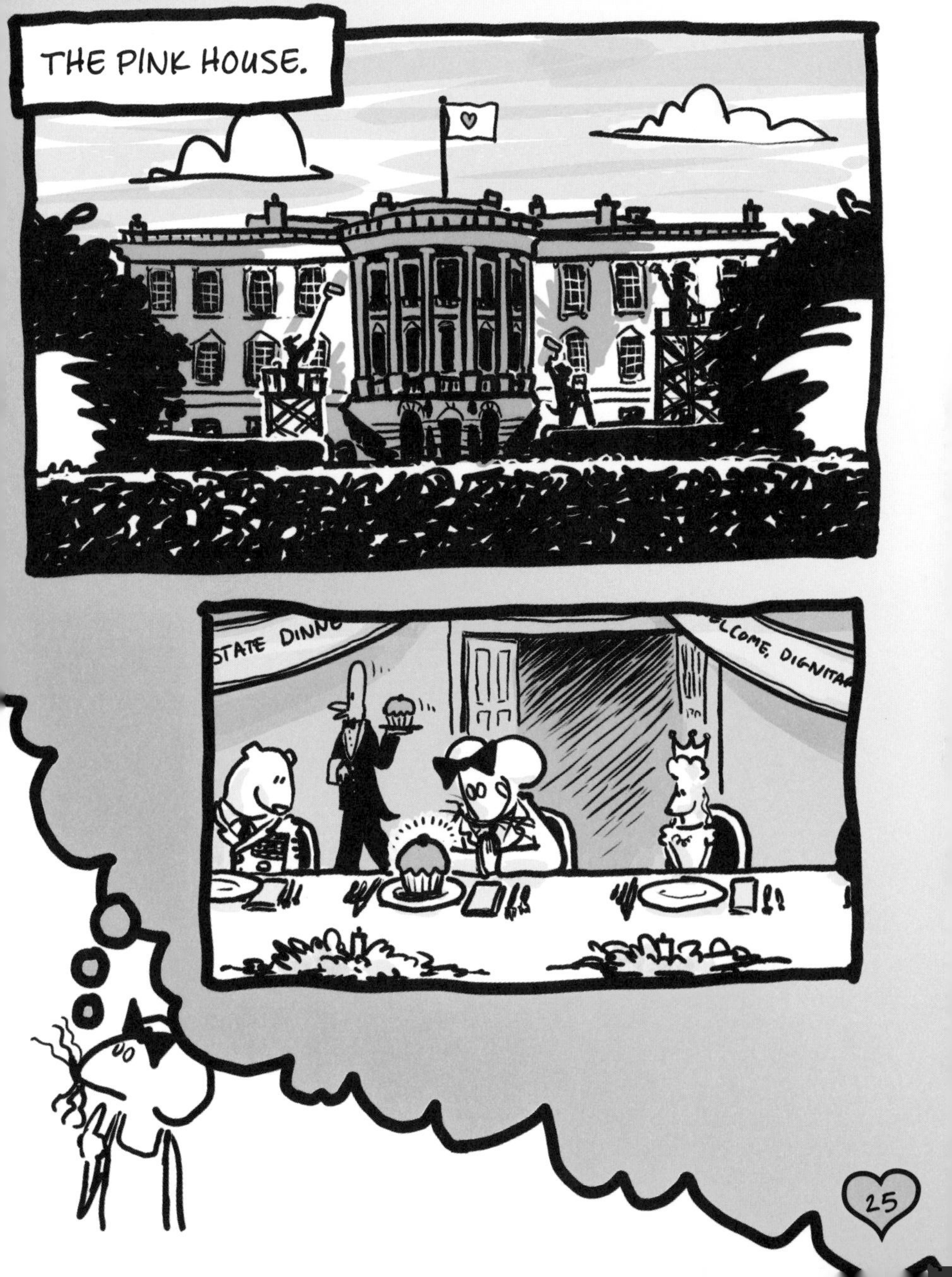
THE PINK HOUSE.
STATE DINN
ELCOME, DIGNITAR

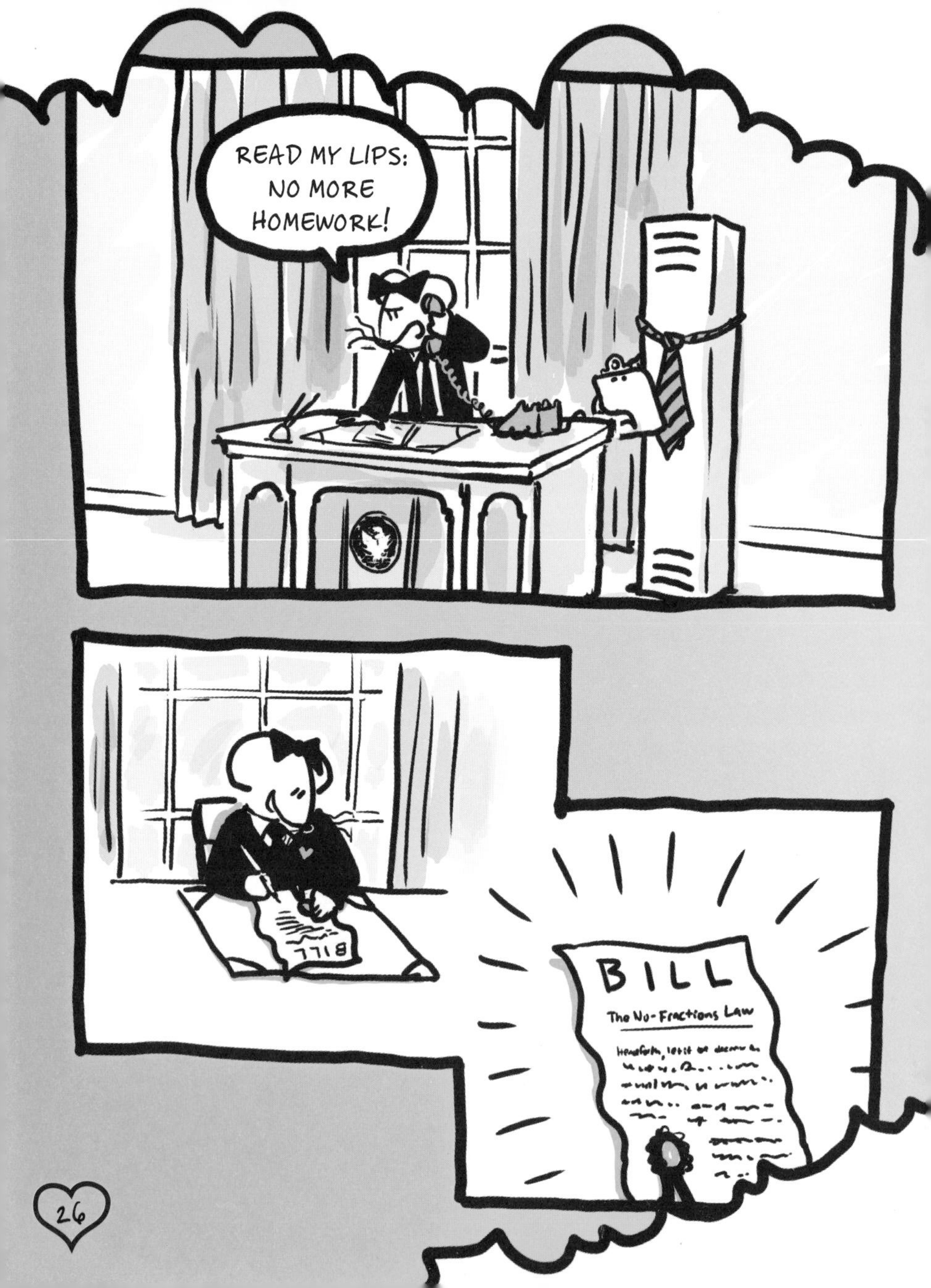
READ MY LIPS: NO MORE HOMEWORK!
BILL
The No-Fractions Law

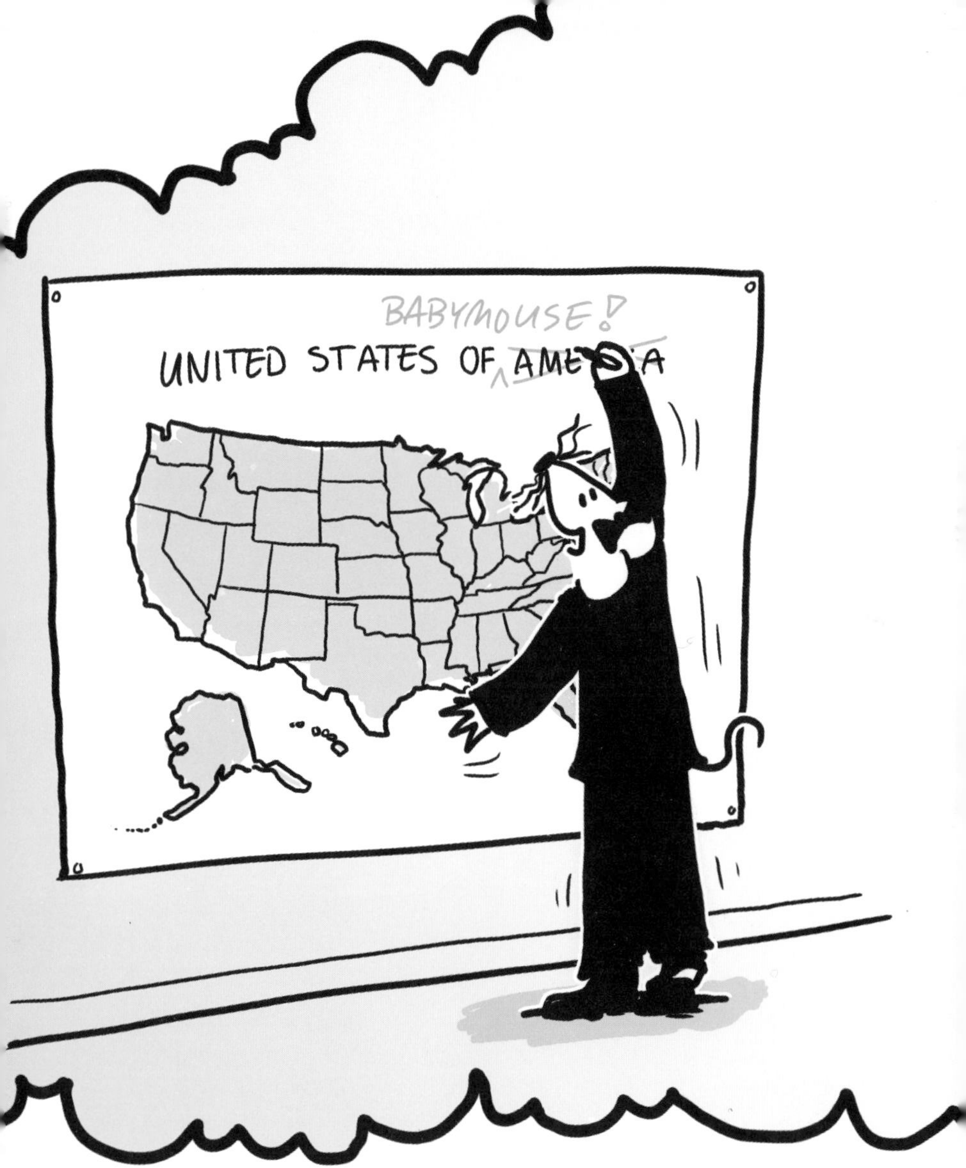
BABYMOUSE!
UNITED STATES OF AME A

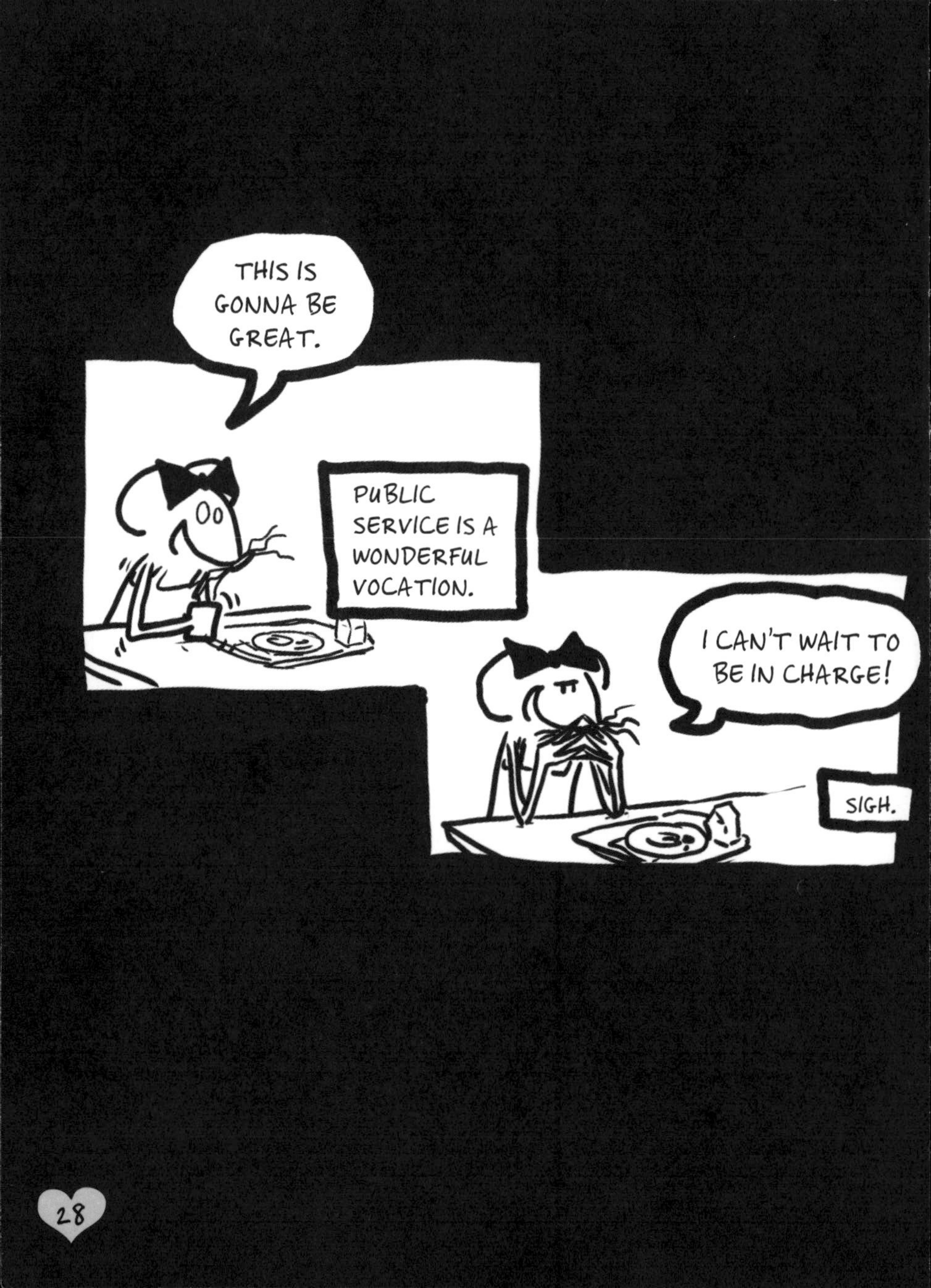
THIS IS GONNA BE GREAT.
PUBLIC SERVICE IS A WONDERFUL VOCATION.
I CAN'T WAIT TO BE IN CHARGE!
SIGH.

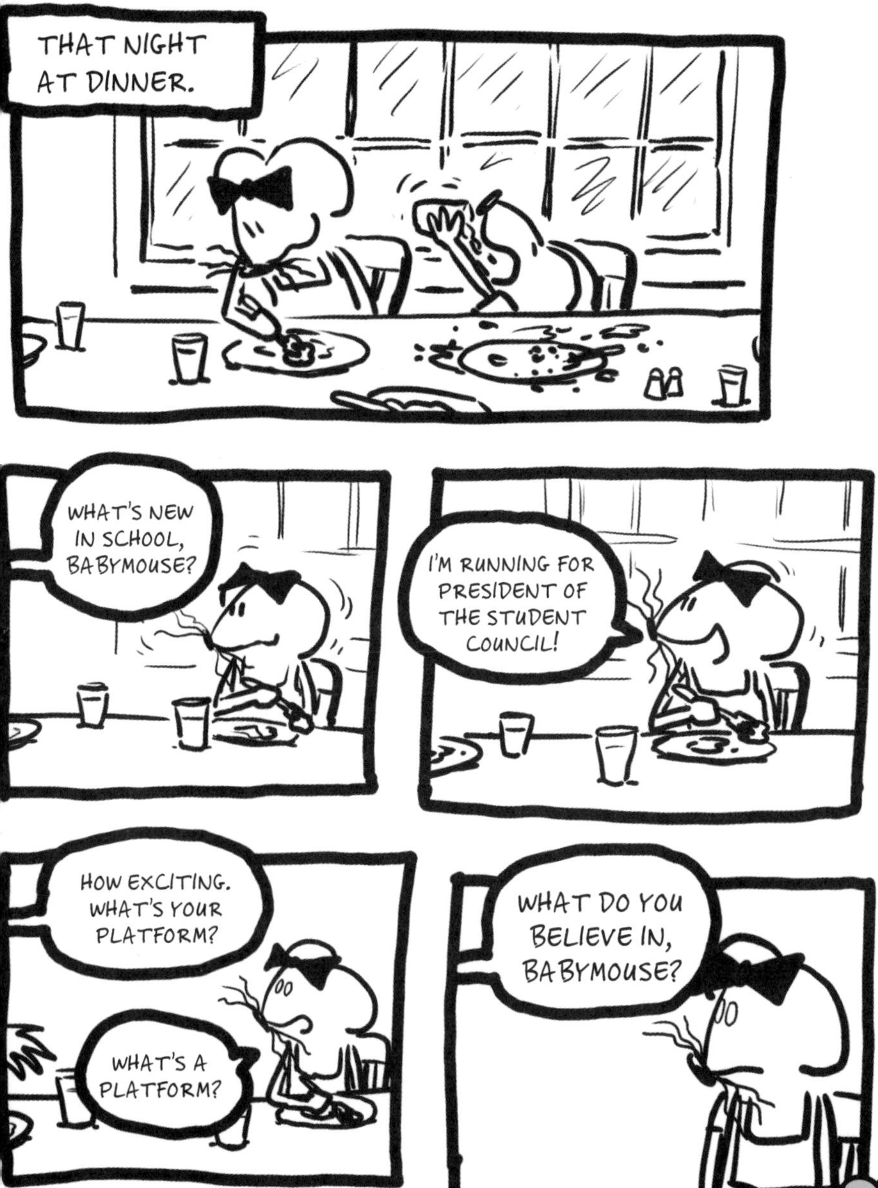
THAT NIGHT AT DINNER.
WHAT'S NEW IN SCHOOL, BABYMOUSE?
I'M RUNNING FOR PRESIDENT OF THE STUDENT COUNCIL!
HOW EXCITING. WHAT'S YOUR PLATFORM?
WHAT'S A PLATFORM?
WHAT DO YOU BELIEVE IN, BABYMOUSE?

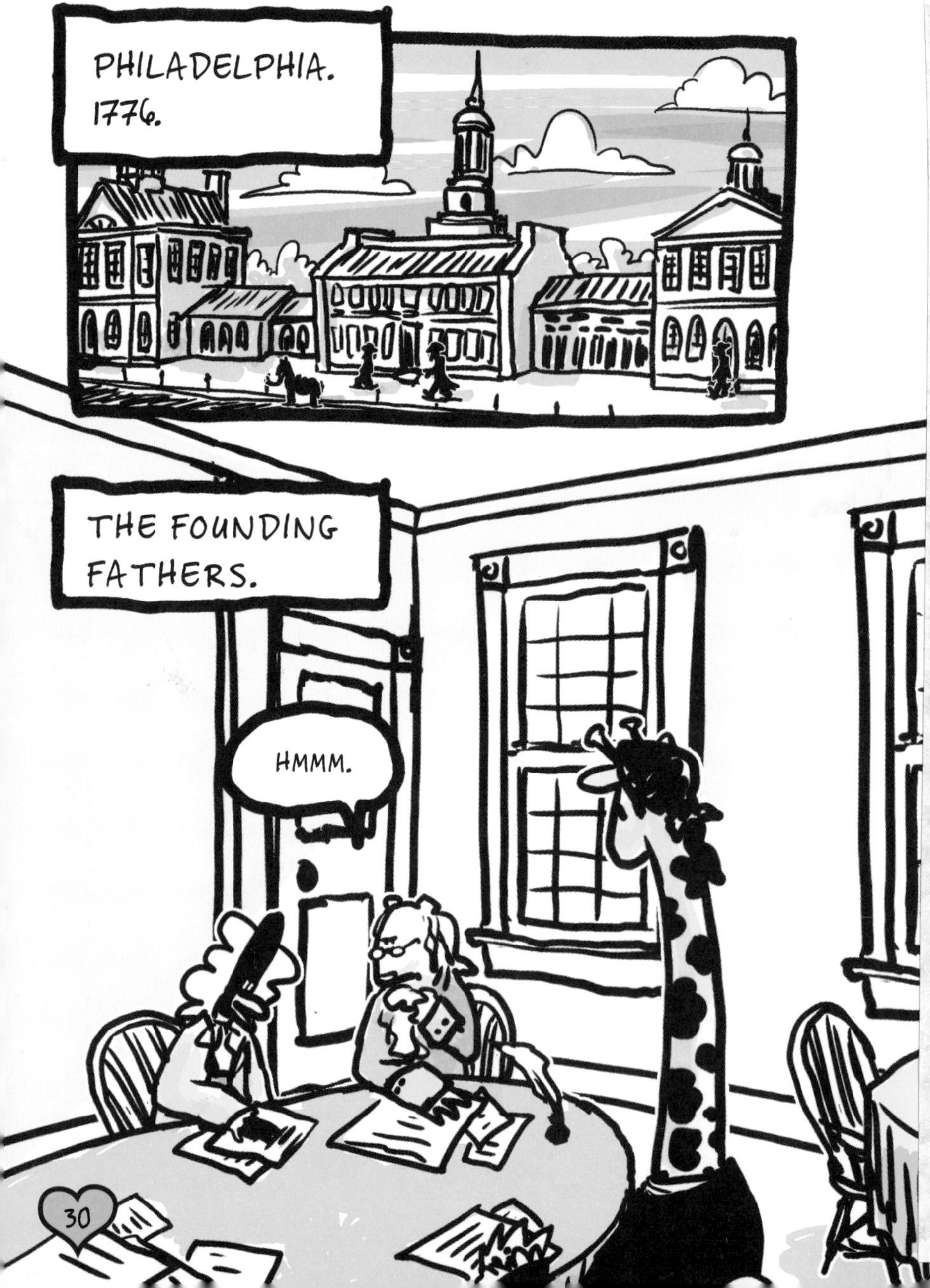
PHILADELPHIA.
1776.
THE FOUNDING FATHERS.
HMMM.

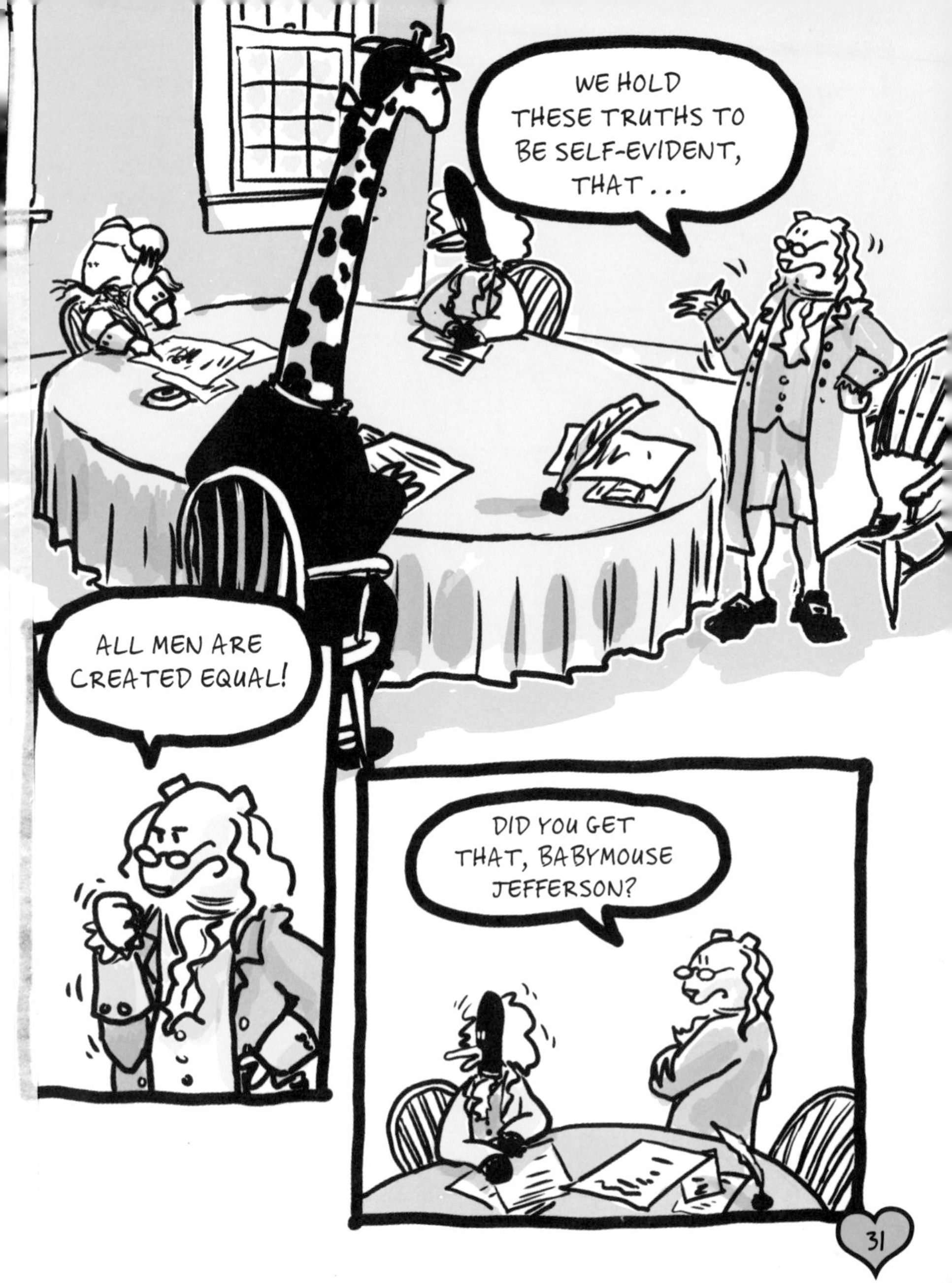
WE HOLD THESE TRUTHS TO BE SELF-EVIDENT, THAT . . .
ALL MEN ARE CREATED EQUAL!
DID YOU GET THAT, BABYMOUSE JEFFERSON?

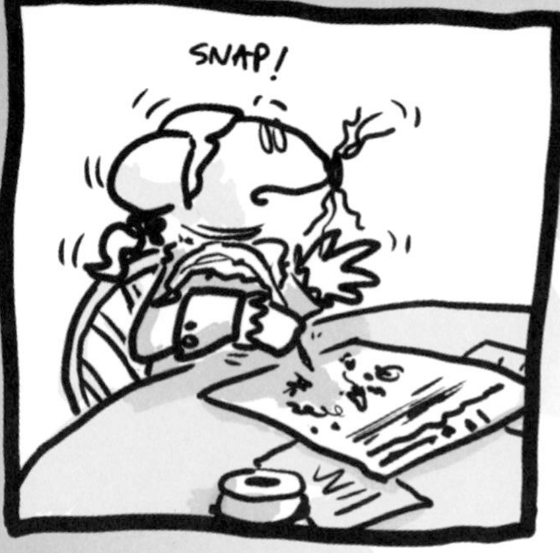
SNAP!

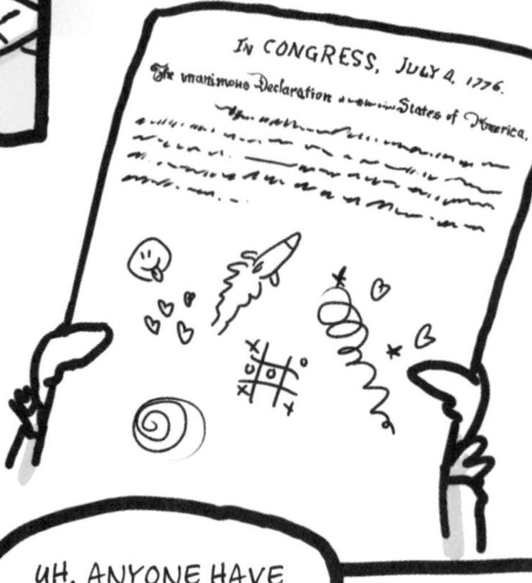
IN CONGRESS, JULY 4, 1776.
The unanimous Declaration
States of America.

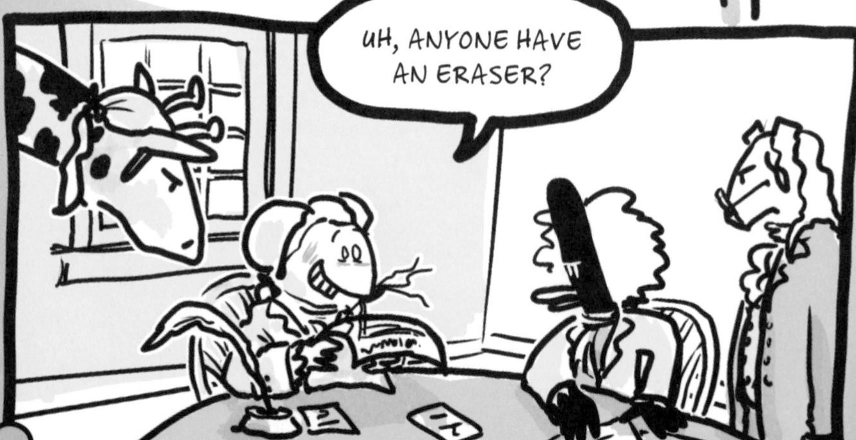
UH, ANYONE HAVE AN ERASER?

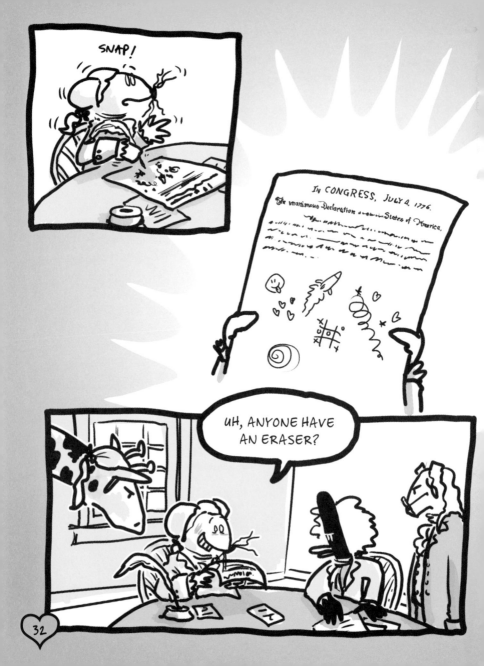

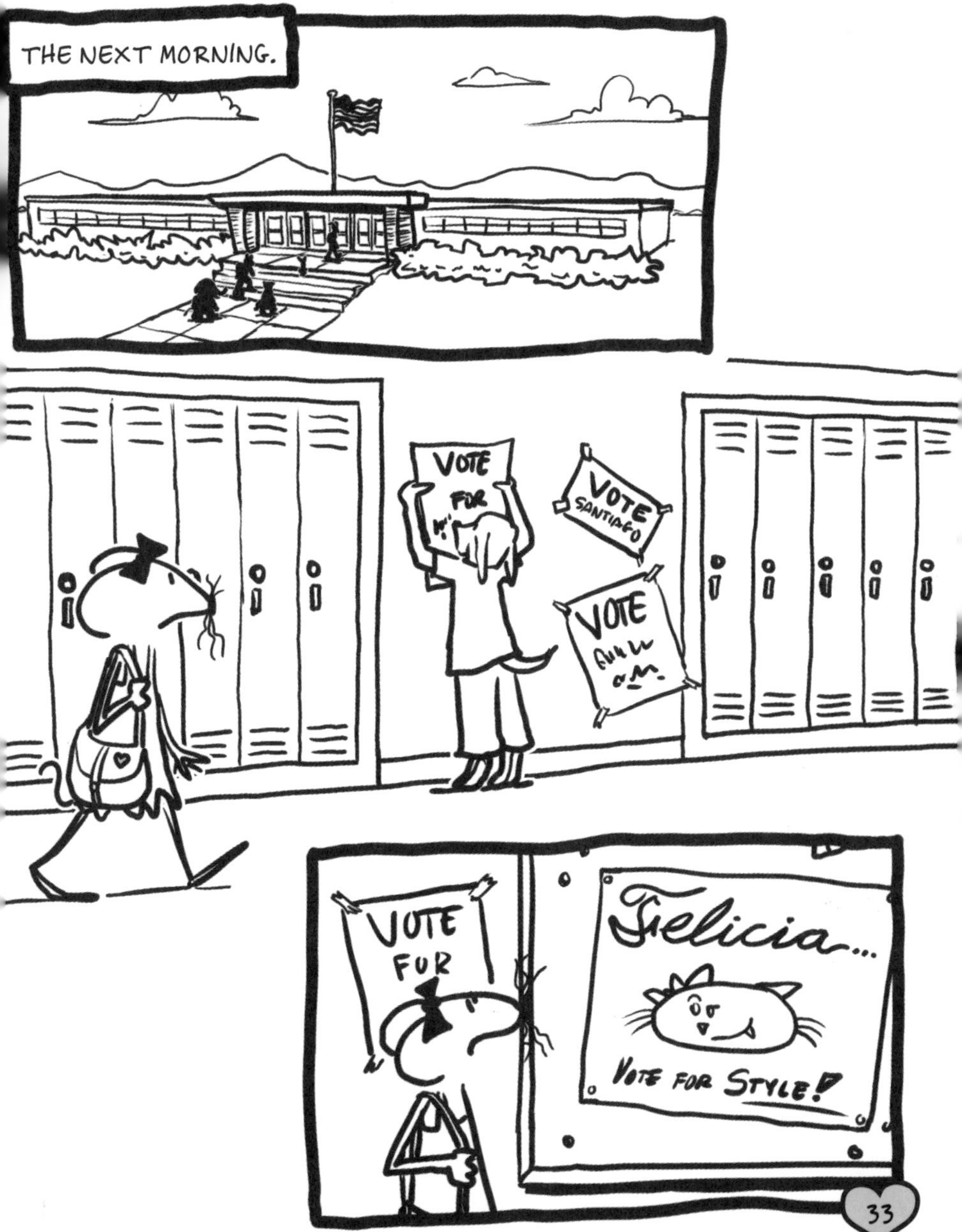
THE NEXT MORNING.
VOTE FOR
VOTE SANTIAGO
VOTE
VOTE FUR
Felicia...
VOTE FOR STYLE!

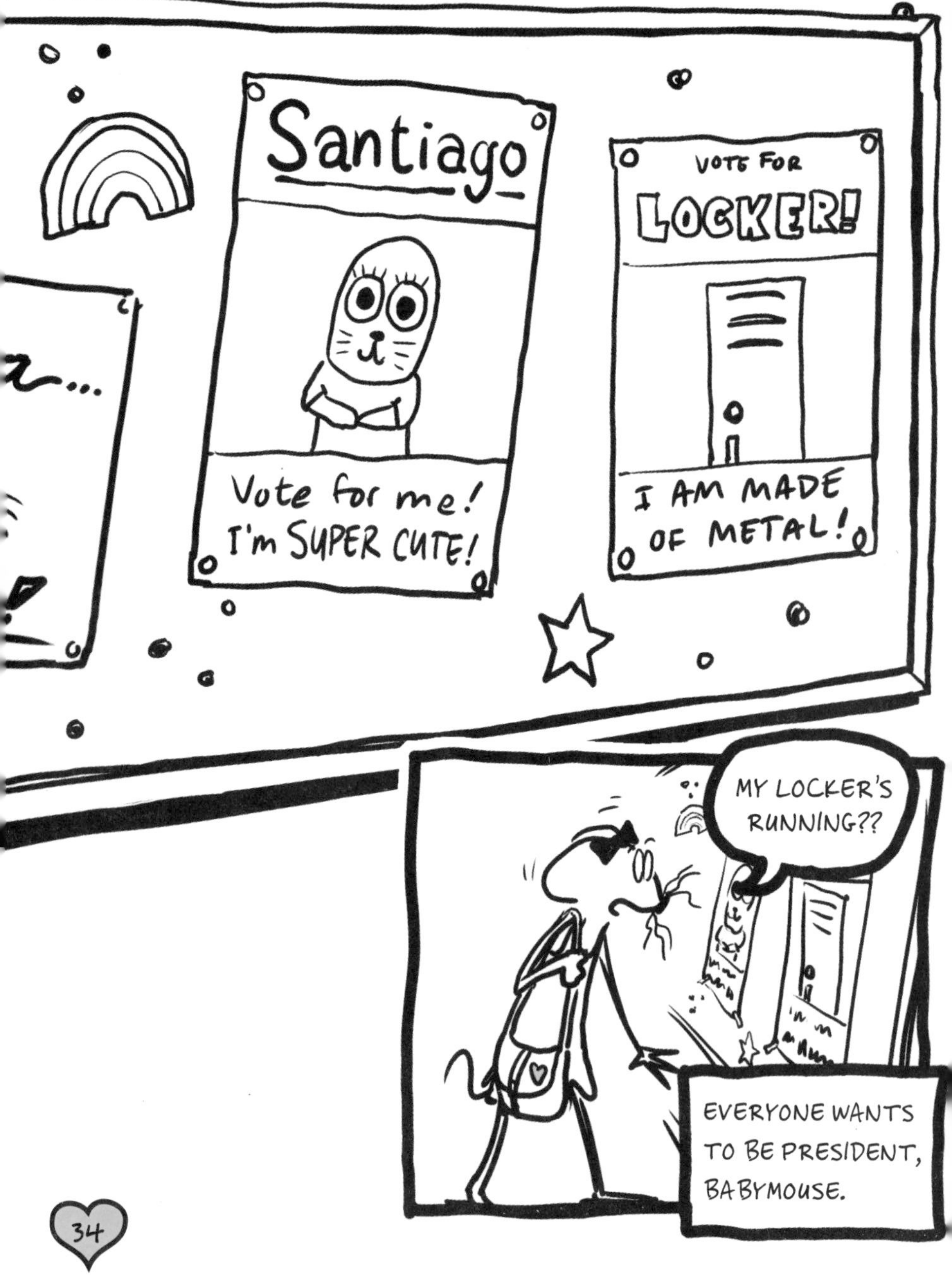
Santiago
Vote for me! I'm SUPER CUTE!
VOTE FOR
LOCKER!
I AM MADE OF METAL!
MY LOCKER'S RUNNING??
EVERYONE WANTS TO BE PRESIDENT, BABYMOUSE.

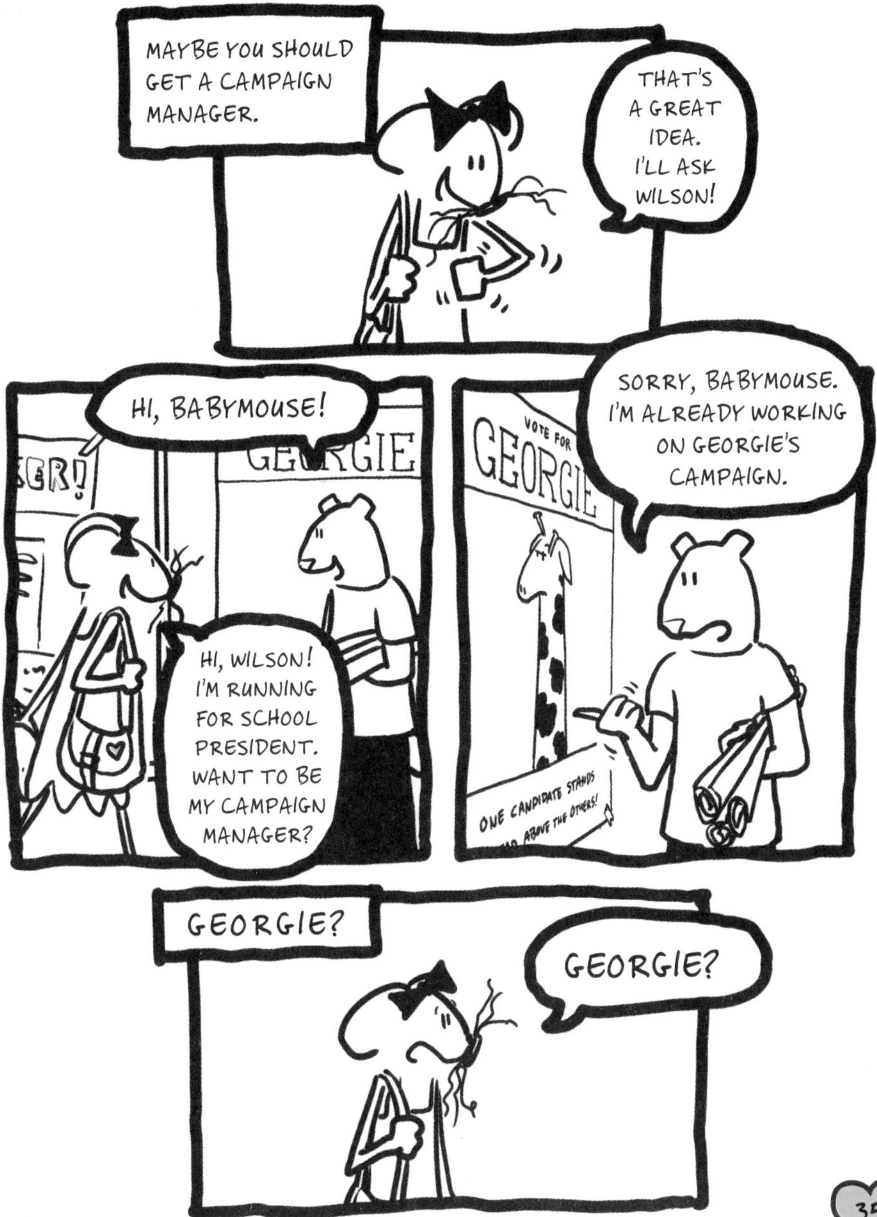
MAYBE YOU SHOULD GET A CAMPAIGN MANAGER.
THAT'S A GREAT IDEA. I'LL ASK WILSON!
HI, BABYMOUSE!
HI, WILSON! I'M RUNNING FOR SCHOOL PRESIDENT. WANT TO BE MY CAMPAIGN MANAGER?
GEORGIE
VOTE FOR GEORGIE
SORRY, BABYMOUSE. I'M ALREADY WORKING ON GEORGIE'S CAMPAIGN.
ONE CANDIDATE STANDS ABOVE THE OTHERS!
GEORGIE?
GEORGIE?

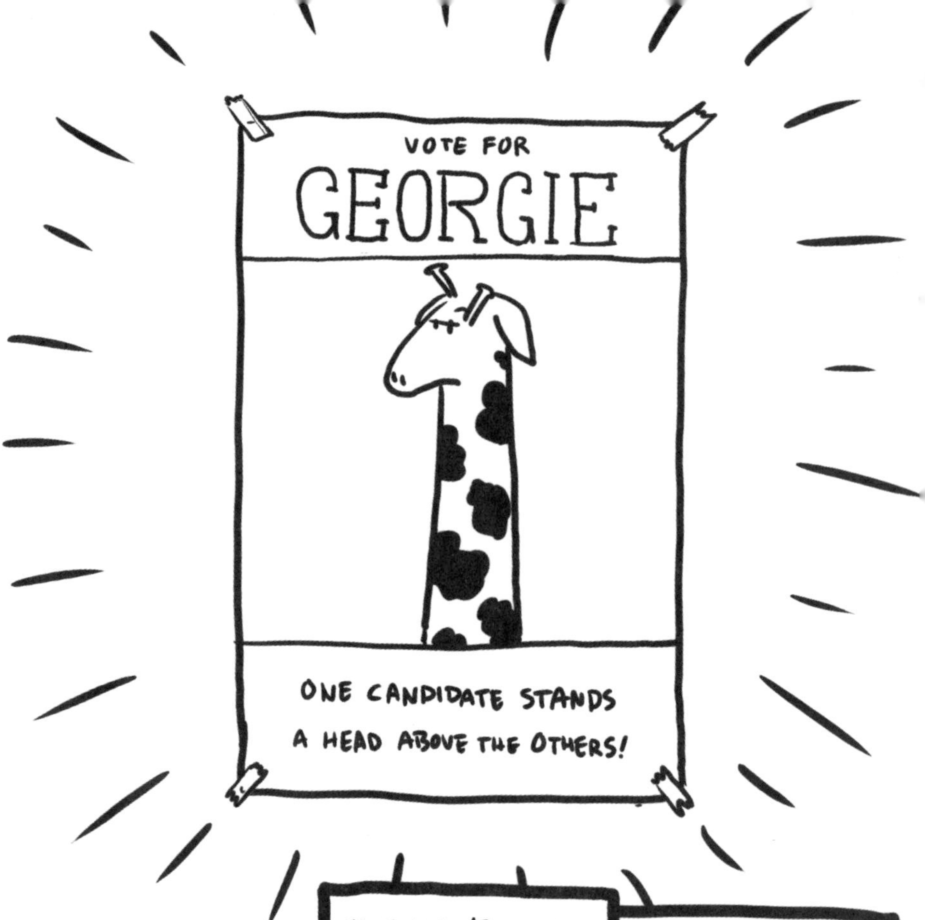
VOTE FOR
GEORGIE
ONE CANDIDATE STANDS
A HEAD ABOVE THE OTHERS!

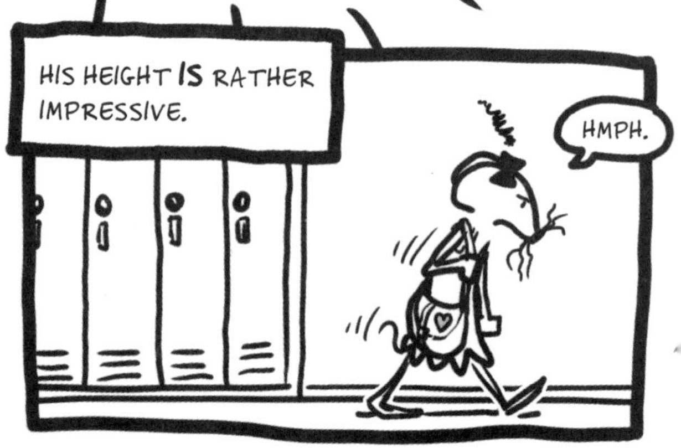
HIS HEIGHT IS RATHER IMPRESSIVE.
HMPH.

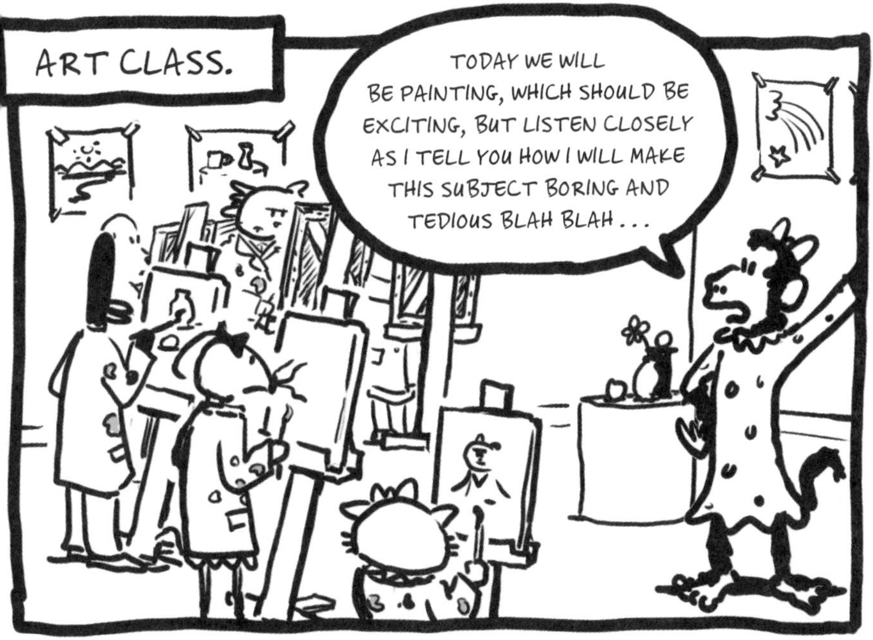
ART CLASS.
TODAY WE WILL BE PAINTING, WHICH SHOULD BE EXCITING, BUT LISTEN CLOSELY AS I TELL YOU HOW I WILL MAKE THIS SUBJECT BORING AND TEDIOUS BLAH BLAH . . .

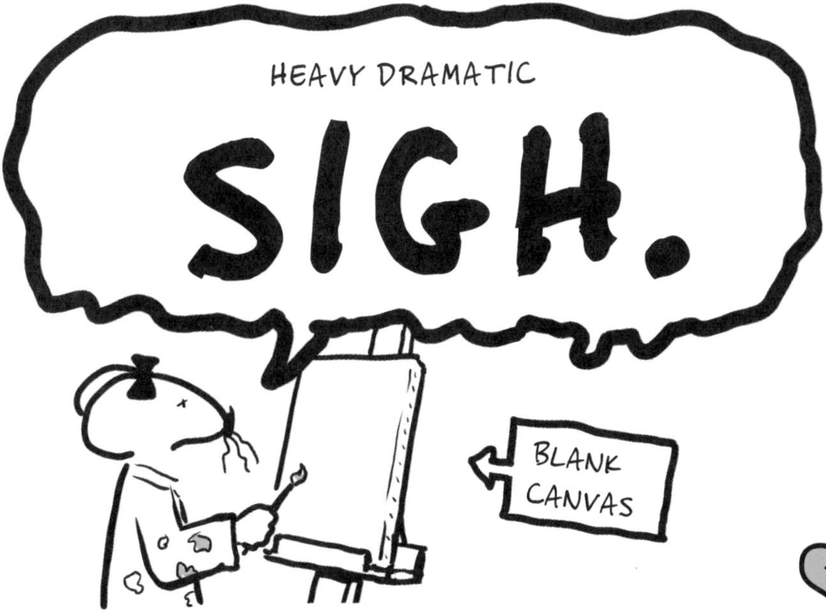
HEAVY DRAMATIC
SIGH.
BLANK CANVAS

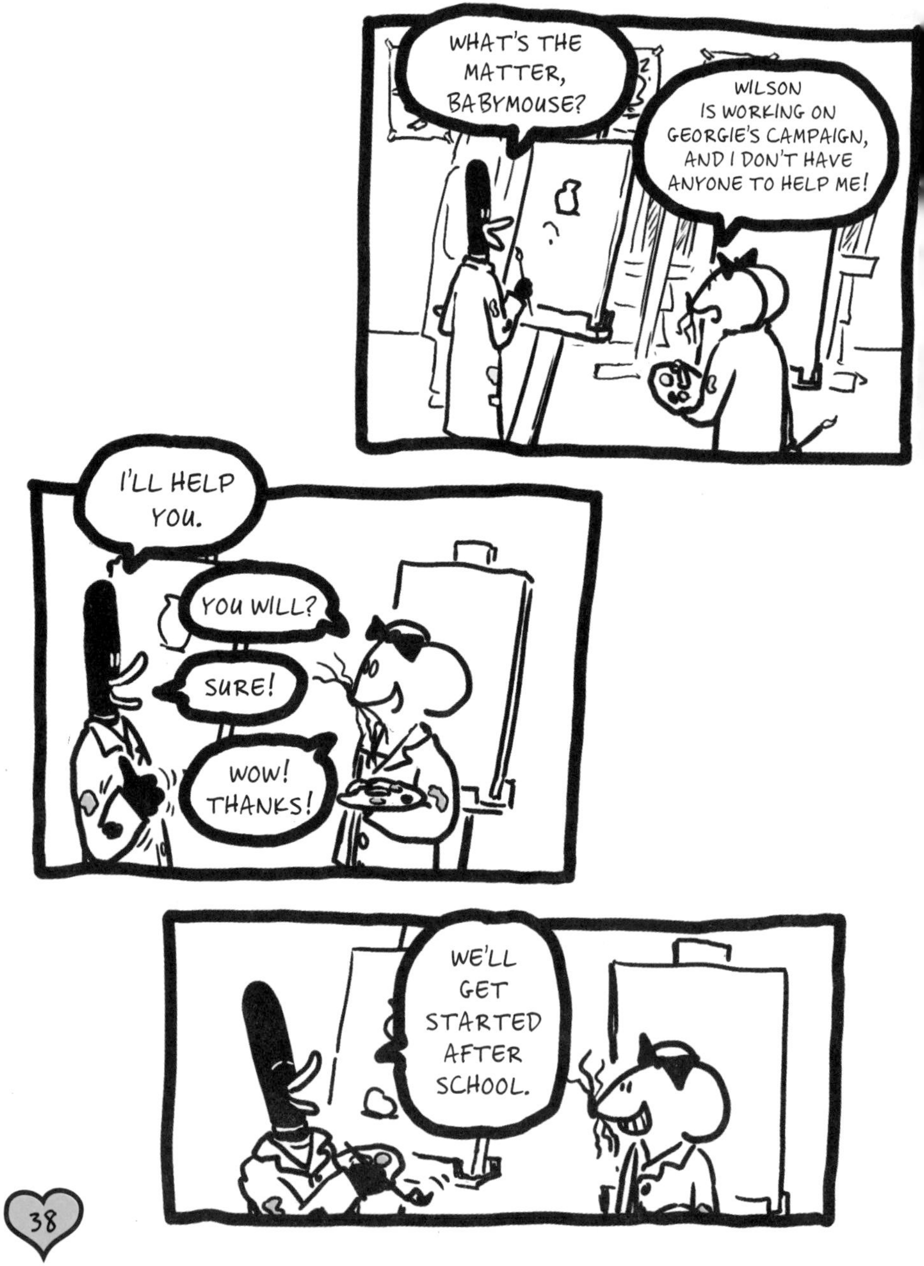
WHAT'S THE MATTER, BABYMOUSE?
WILSON IS WORKING ON GEORGIE'S CAMPAIGN, AND I DON'T HAVE ANYONE TO HELP ME!
I'LL HELP YOU.
YOU WILL?
SURE!
WOW! THANKS!
WE'LL GET STARTED AFTER SCHOOL.

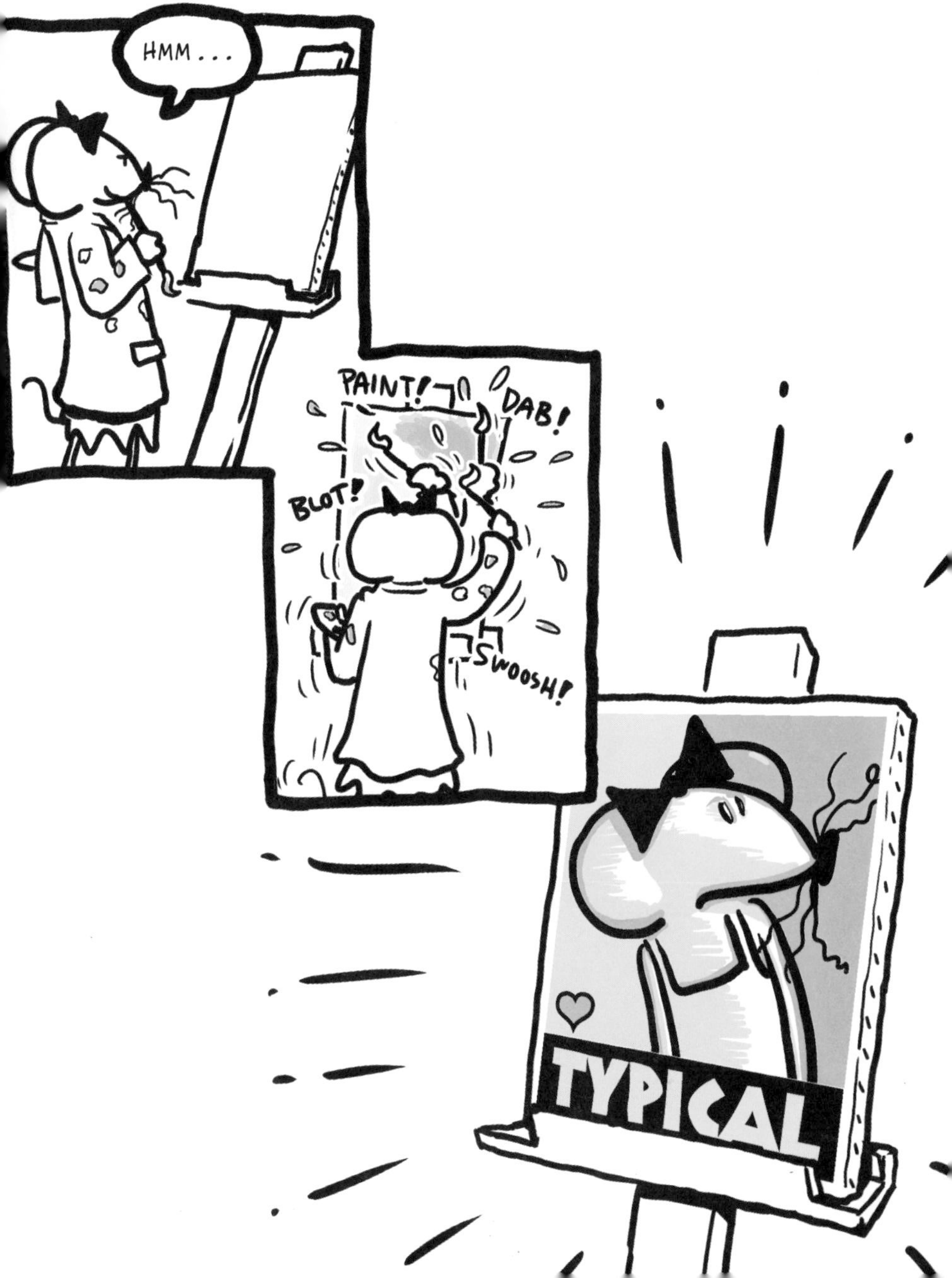
HMM...
PAINT!
DAB!
BLOT!
SWOOSH!
TYPICAL

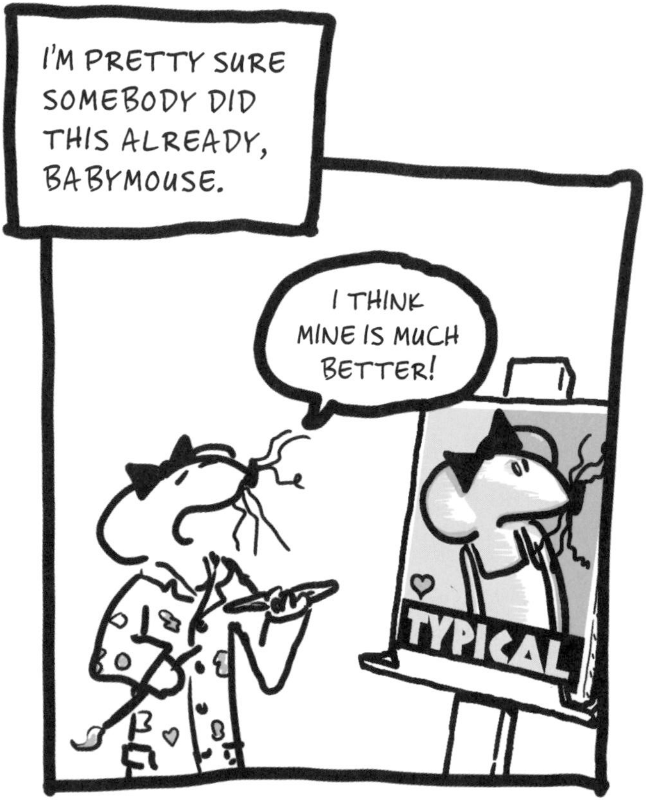
I'M PRETTY SURE SOMEBODY DID THIS ALREADY, BABYMOUSE.
I THINK MINE IS MUCH BETTER!
TYPICAL

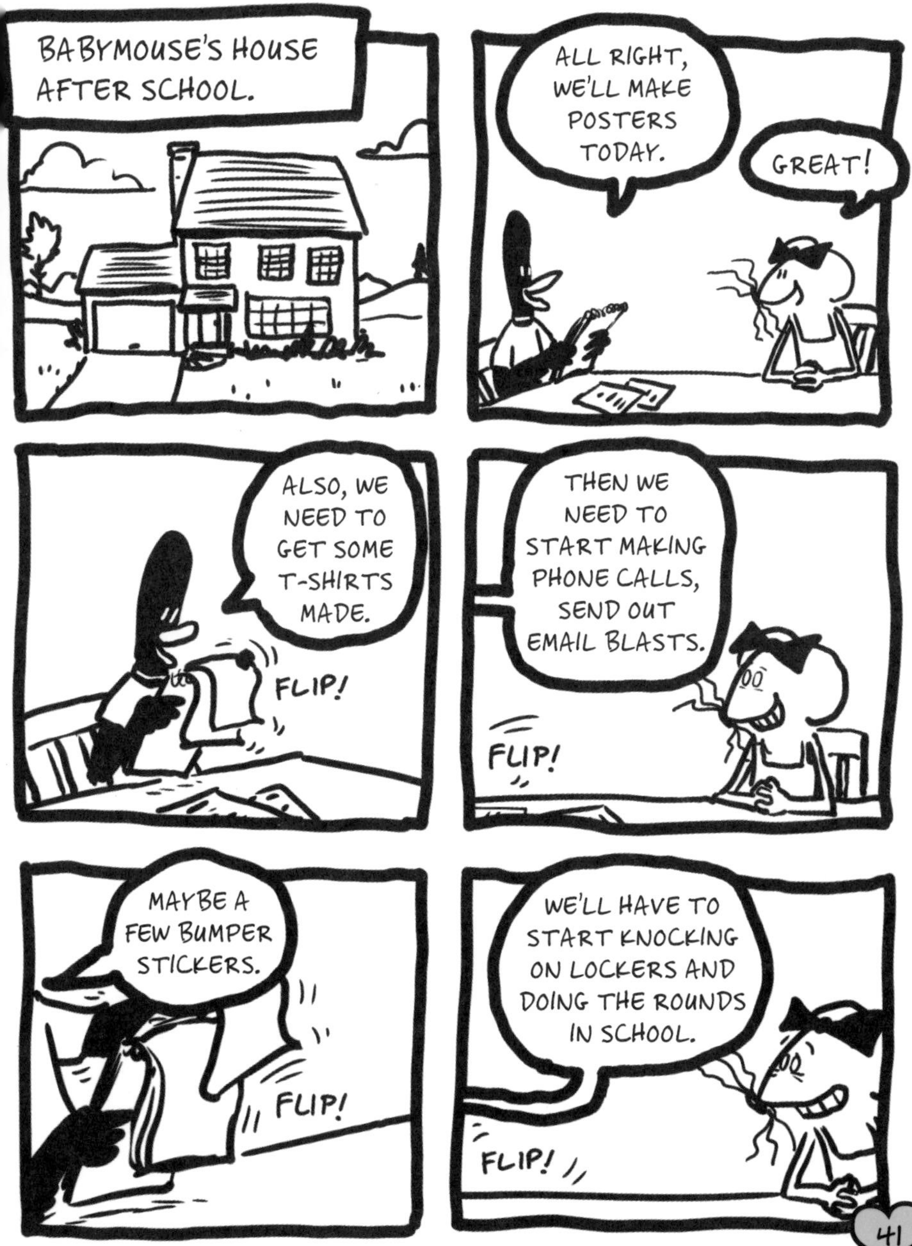
BABYMOUSE'S HOUSE AFTER SCHOOL.
ALL RIGHT, WE'LL MAKE POSTERS TODAY.
GREAT!
ALSO, WE NEED TO GET SOME T-SHIRTS MADE.
FLIP!
THEN WE NEED TO START MAKING PHONE CALLS, SEND OUT EMAIL BLASTS.
FLIP!
MAYBE A FEW BUMPER STICKERS.
FLIP!
WE'LL HAVE TO START KNOCKING ON LOCKERS AND DOING THE ROUNDS IN SCHOOL.
FLIP!

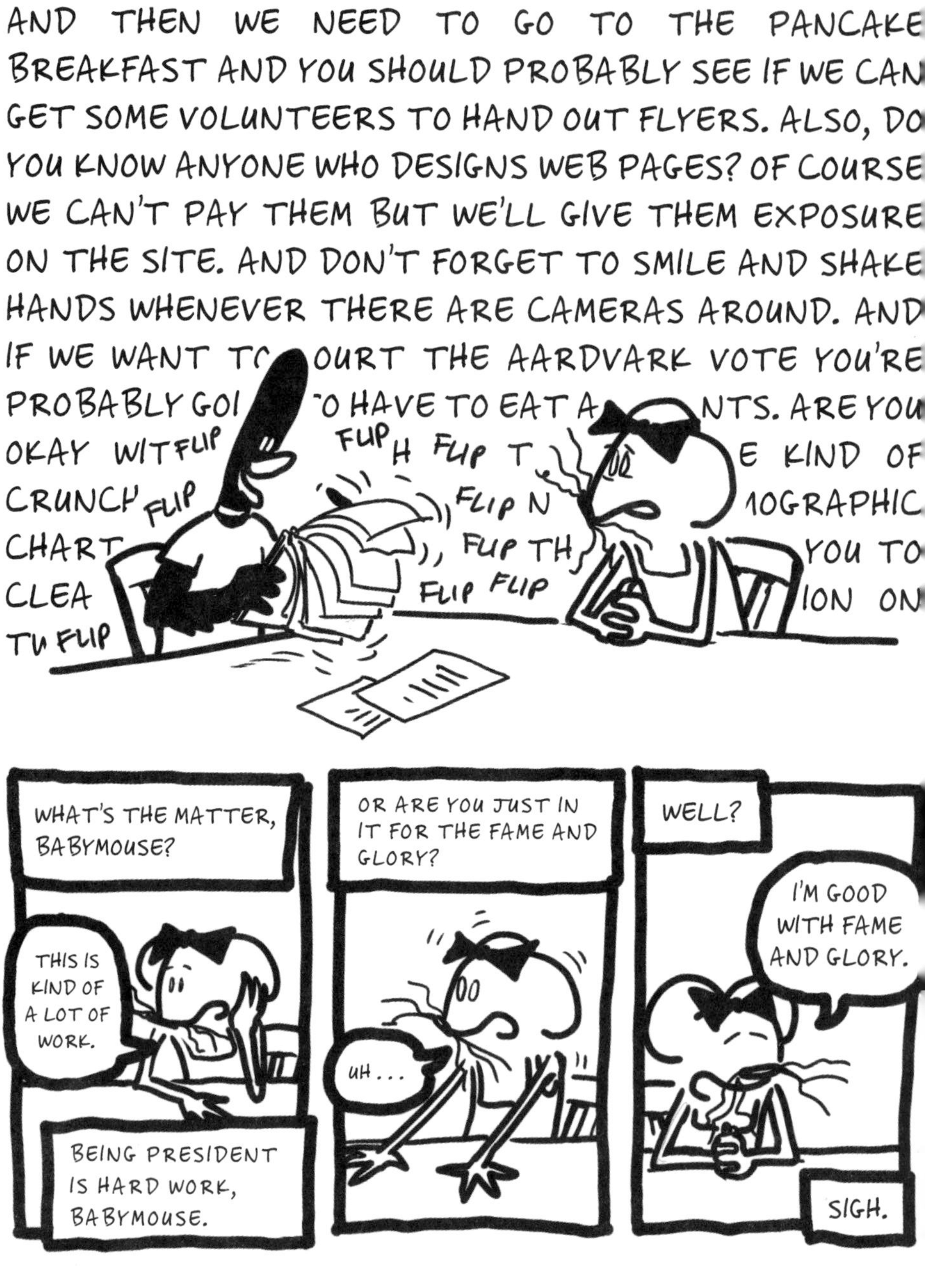
AND THEN WE NEED TO GO TO THE PANCAKE
BREAKFAST AND YOU SHOULD PROBABLY SEE IF WE CAN
GET SOME VOLUNTEERS TO HAND OUT FLYERS. ALSO, DO
YOU KNOW ANYONE WHO DESIGNS WEB PAGES? OF COURSE
WE CAN'T PAY THEM BUT WE'LL GIVE THEM EXPOSURE
ON THE SITE. AND DON'T FORGET TO SMILE AND SHAKE
HANDS WHENEVER THERE ARE CAMERAS AROUND. AND
IF WE WANT TO OURT THE AARDVARK VOTE YOU'RE
PROBABLY GOI O HAVE TO EAT A NTS. ARE YOU
OKAY WIT H T E KIND OF
CRUNCH N OGRAPHIC
CHART TH YOU TO
CLEA ION ON
TU
FLIP FLIP FLIP FLIP FLIP FLIP FLIP FLIP FLIP
WHAT'S THE MATTER, BABYMOUSE?
THIS IS KIND OF A LOT OF WORK.
BEING PRESIDENT IS HARD WORK, BABYMOUSE.
OR ARE YOU JUST IN IT FOR THE FAME AND GLORY?
UH...
WELL?
I'M GOOD WITH FAME AND GLORY.
SIGH.

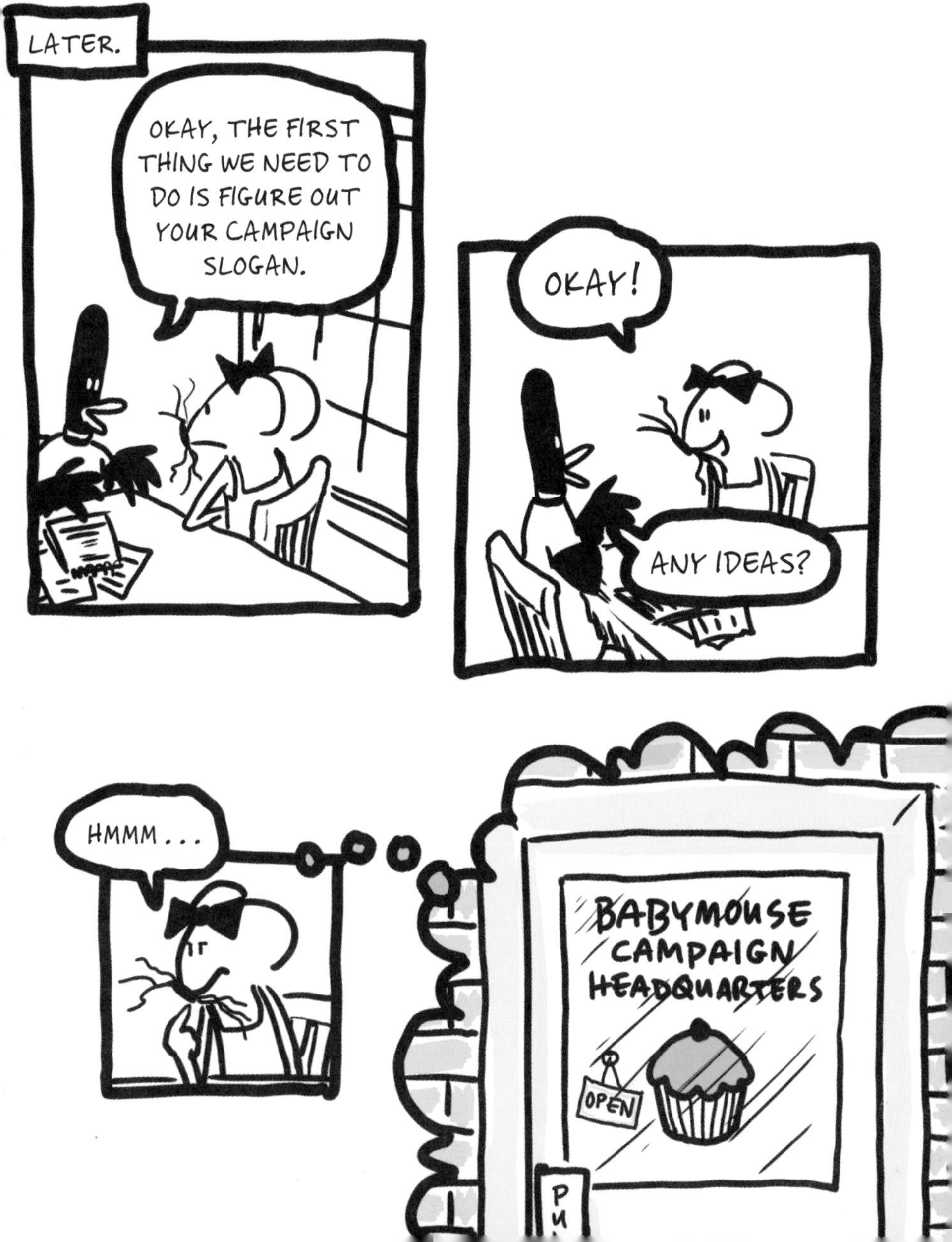
LATER.
OKAY, THE FIRST THING WE NEED TO DO IS FIGURE OUT YOUR CAMPAIGN SLOGAN.
OKAY!
ANY IDEAS?
HMMM...
BABYMOUSE CAMPAIGN HEADQUARTERS
OPEN

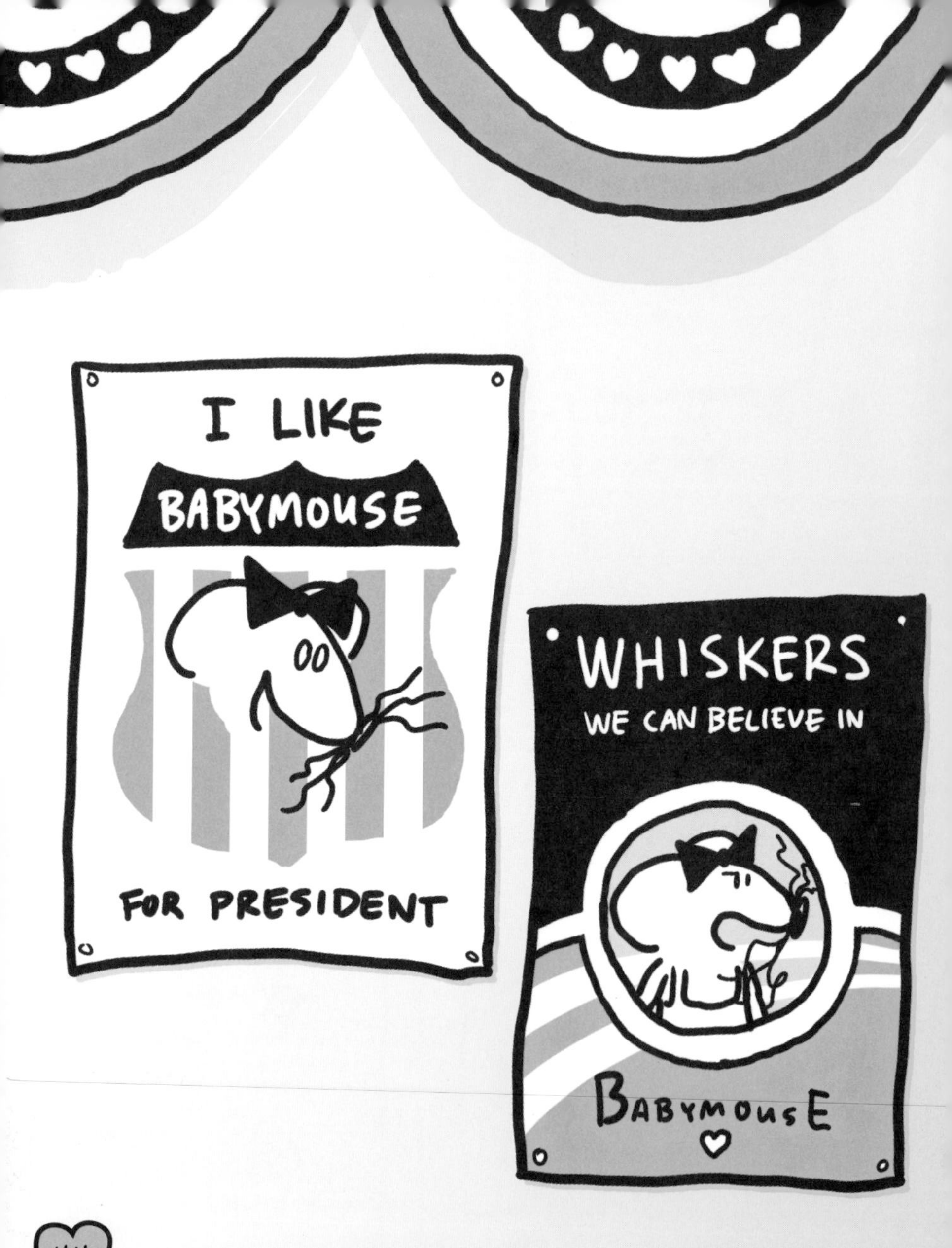
I LIKE
BABYMOUSE
FOR PRESIDENT
WHISKERS
WE CAN BELIEVE IN
BABYMOUSE

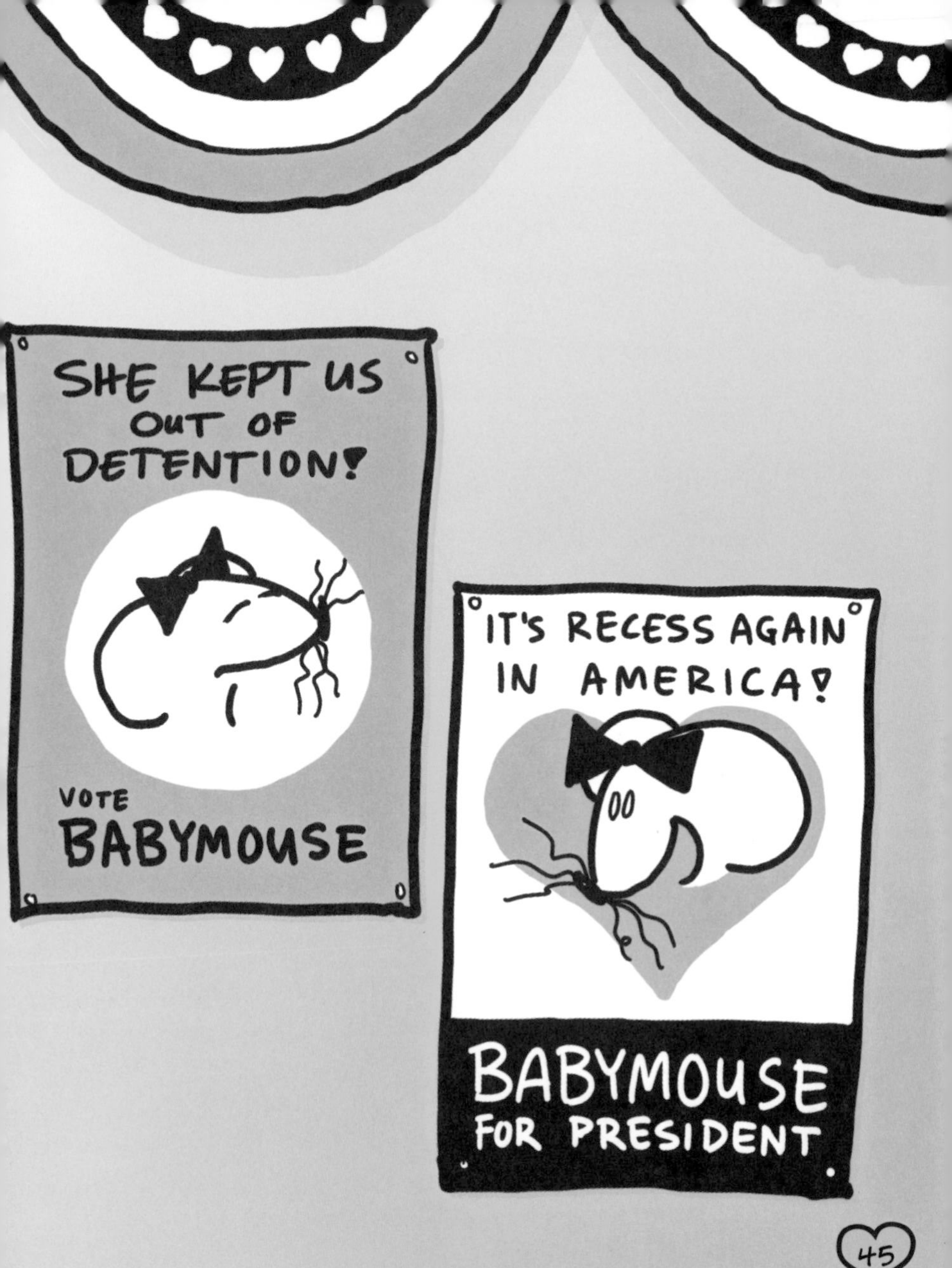
SHE KEPT US OUT OF DETENTION!
VOTE BABYMOUSE
IT'S RECESS AGAIN IN AMERICA!
BABYMOUSE FOR PRESIDENT

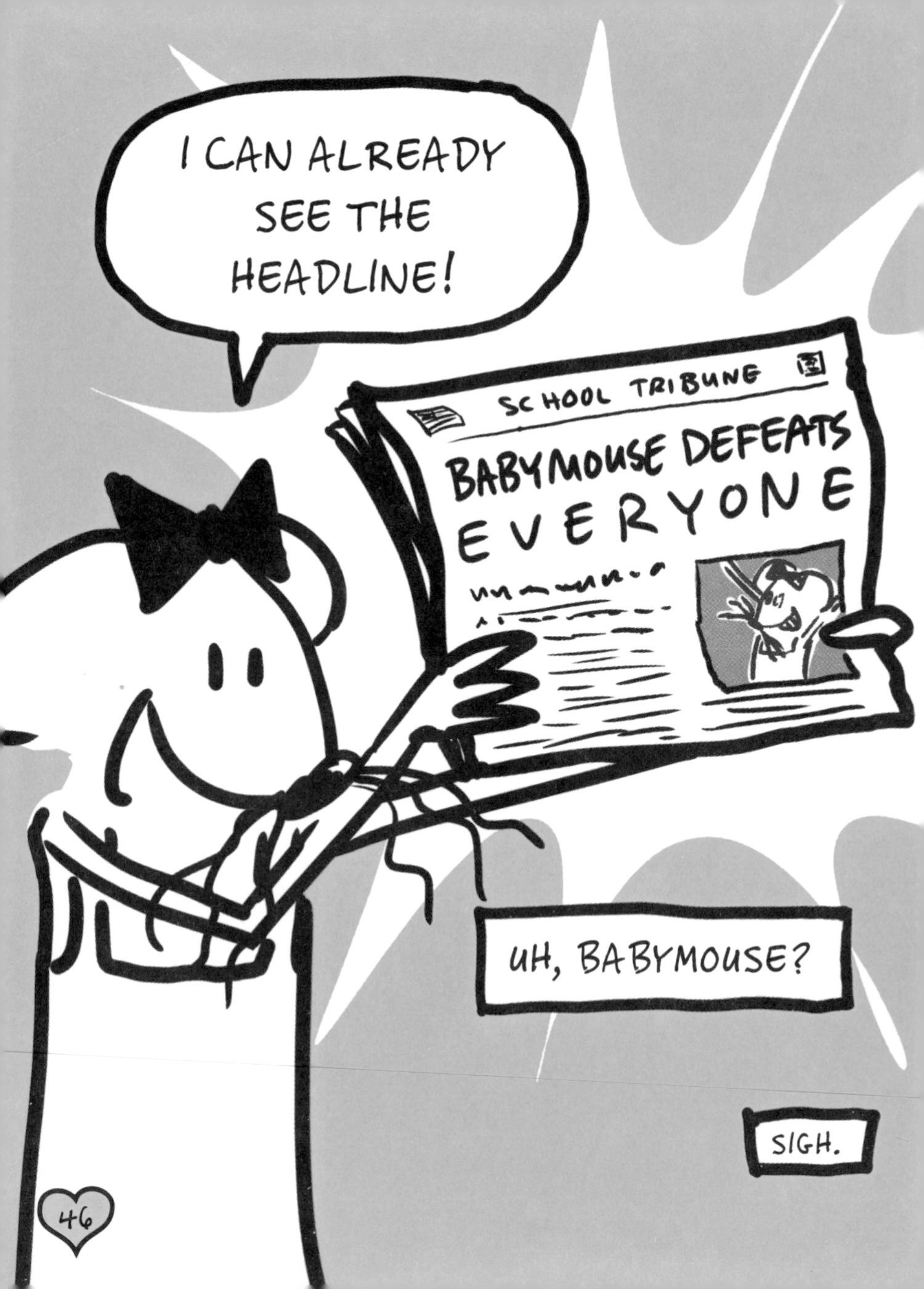
I CAN ALREADY SEE THE HEADLINE!
SCHOOL TRIBUNE
BABYMOUSE DEFEATS EVERYONE
UH, BABYMOUSE?
SIGH.

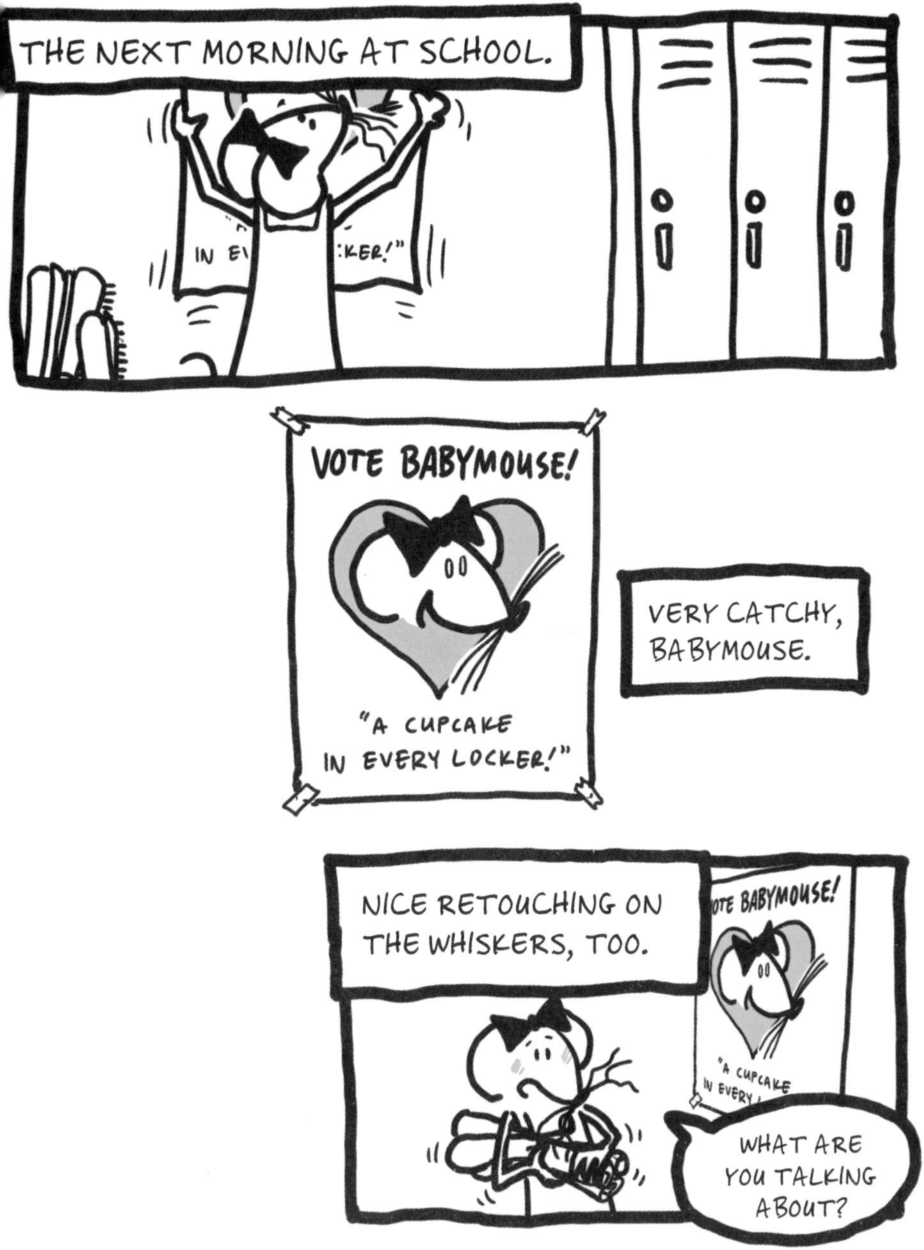
THE NEXT MORNING AT SCHOOL.
VOTE BABYMOUSE!
"A CUPCAKE IN EVERY LOCKER!"
VERY CATCHY, BABYMOUSE.
NICE RETOUCHING ON THE WHISKERS, TOO.
WHAT ARE YOU TALKING ABOUT?

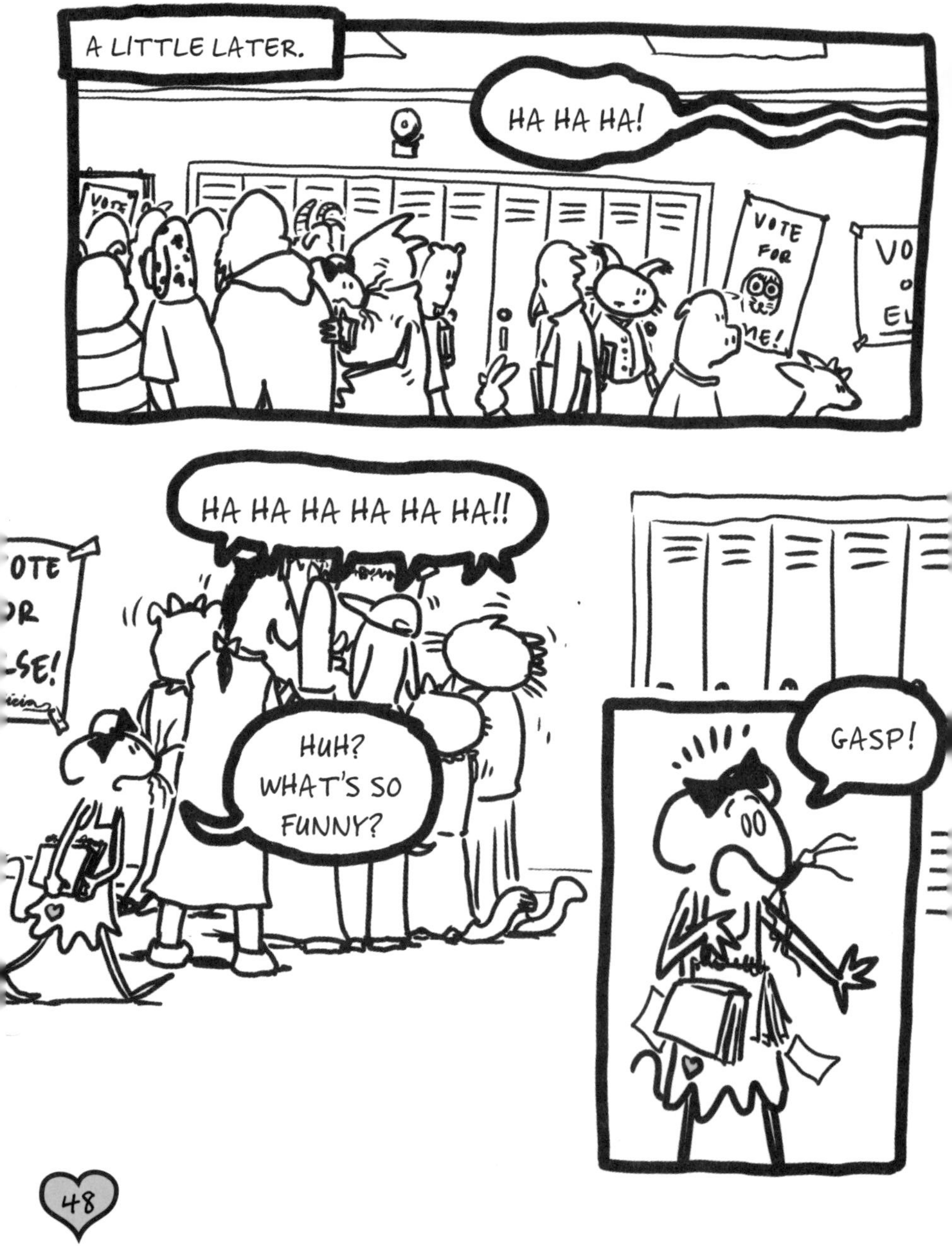
A LITTLE LATER.
HA HA HA!
HA HA HA HA HA HA!!
HUH? WHAT'S SO FUNNY?
GASP!

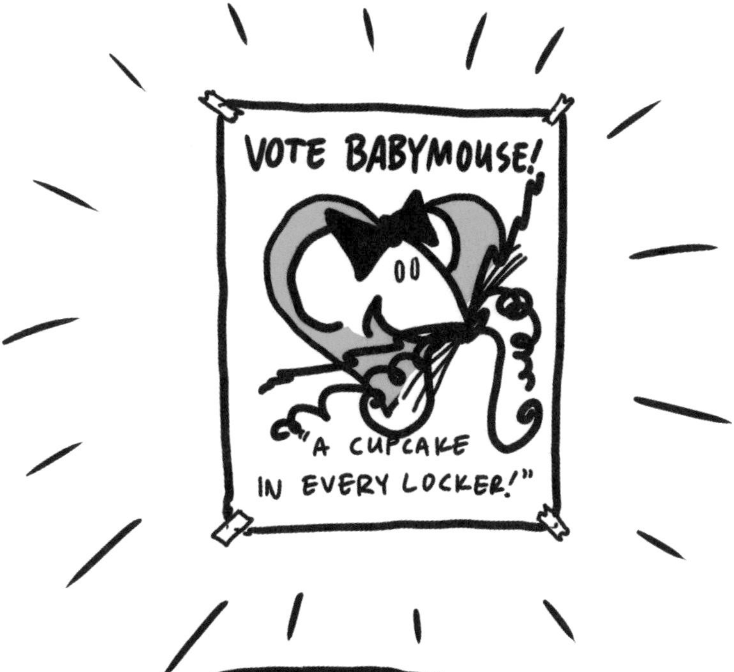
VOTE BABYMOUSE!
"A CUPCAKE
IN EVERY LOCKER!"

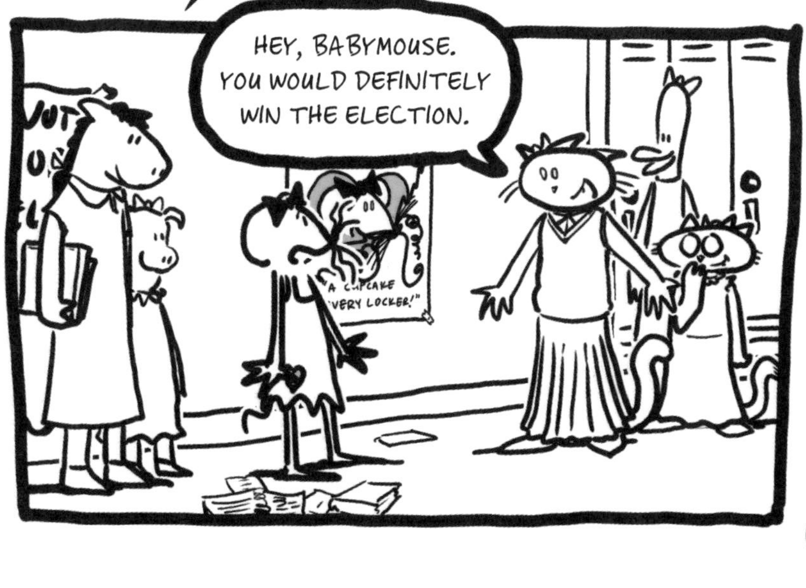
HEY, BABYMOUSE. YOU WOULD DEFINITELY WIN THE ELECTION.

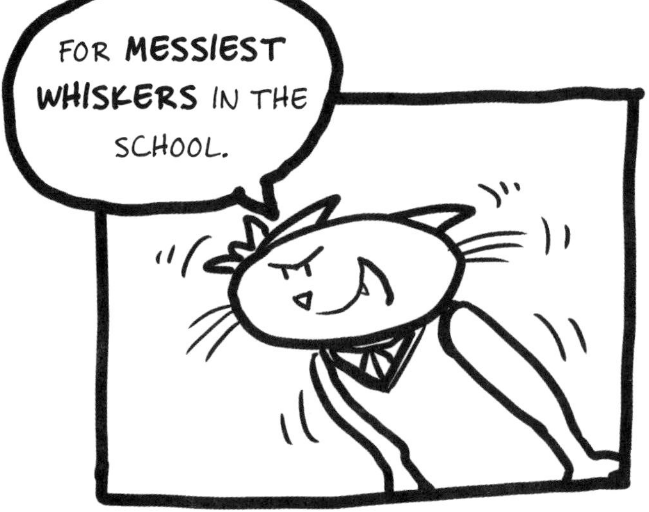
FOR MESSIEST WHISKERS IN THE SCHOOL.

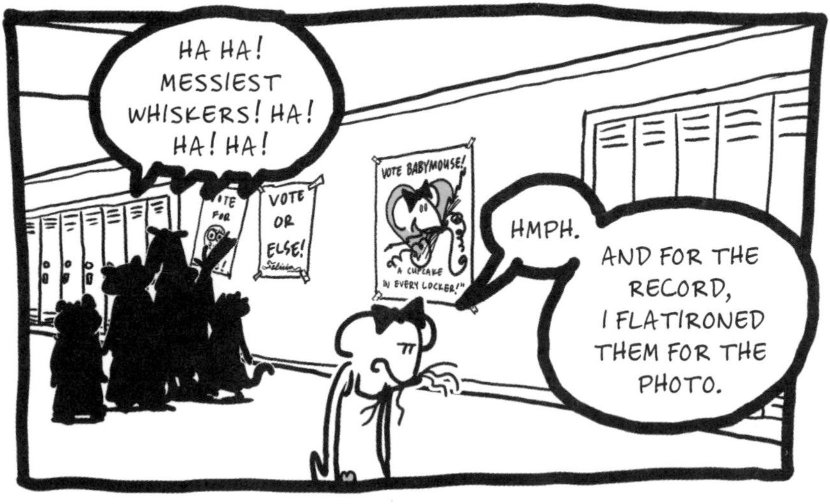
HA HA! MESSIEST WHISKERS! HA! HA! HA!
VOTE OR ELSE!
VOTE BABYMOUSE!
"A CUPCAKE IN EVERY LOCKER!"
HMPH.
AND FOR THE RECORD, I FLATIRONED THEM FOR THE PHOTO.

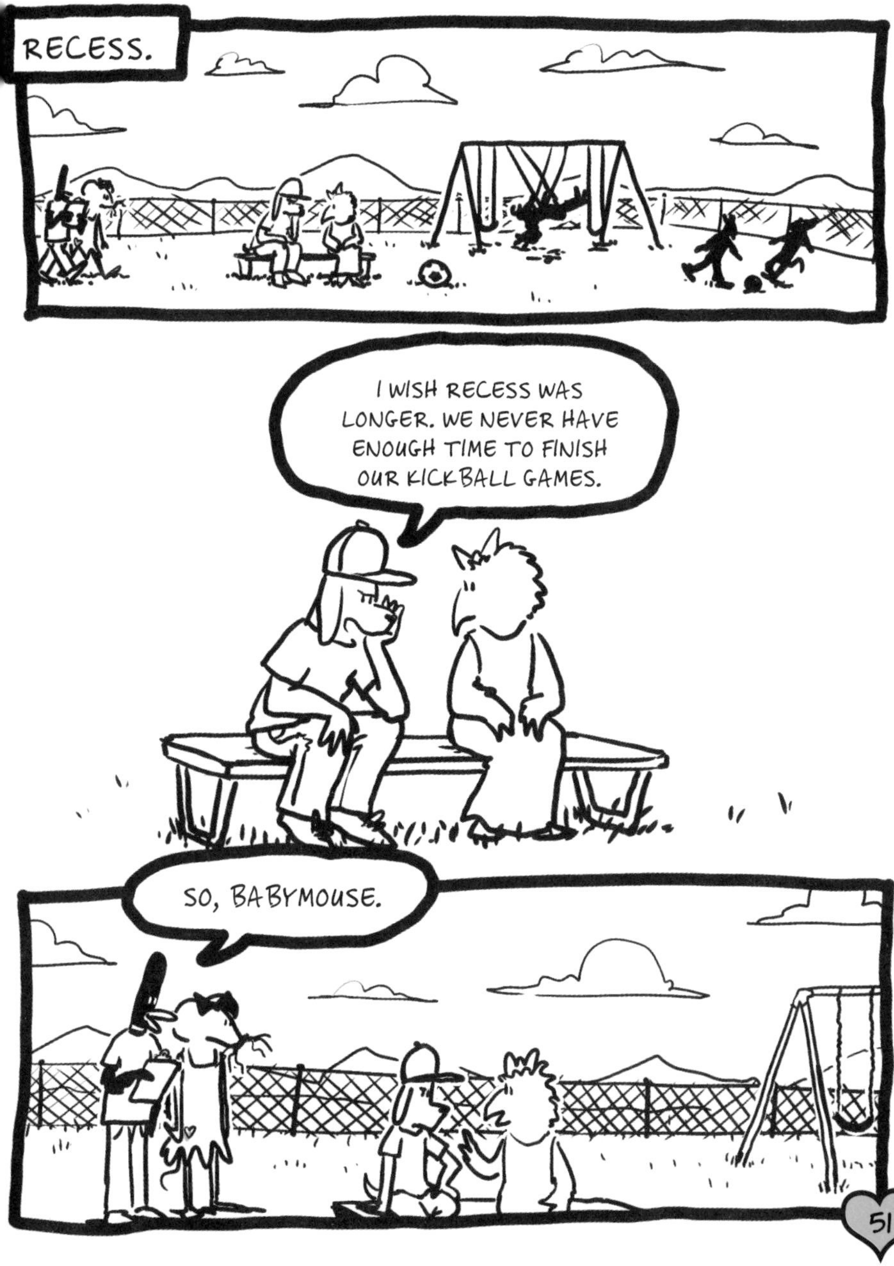
RECESS.
I WISH RECESS WAS LONGER. WE NEVER HAVE ENOUGH TIME TO FINISH OUR KICKBALL GAMES.
SO, BABYMOUSE.

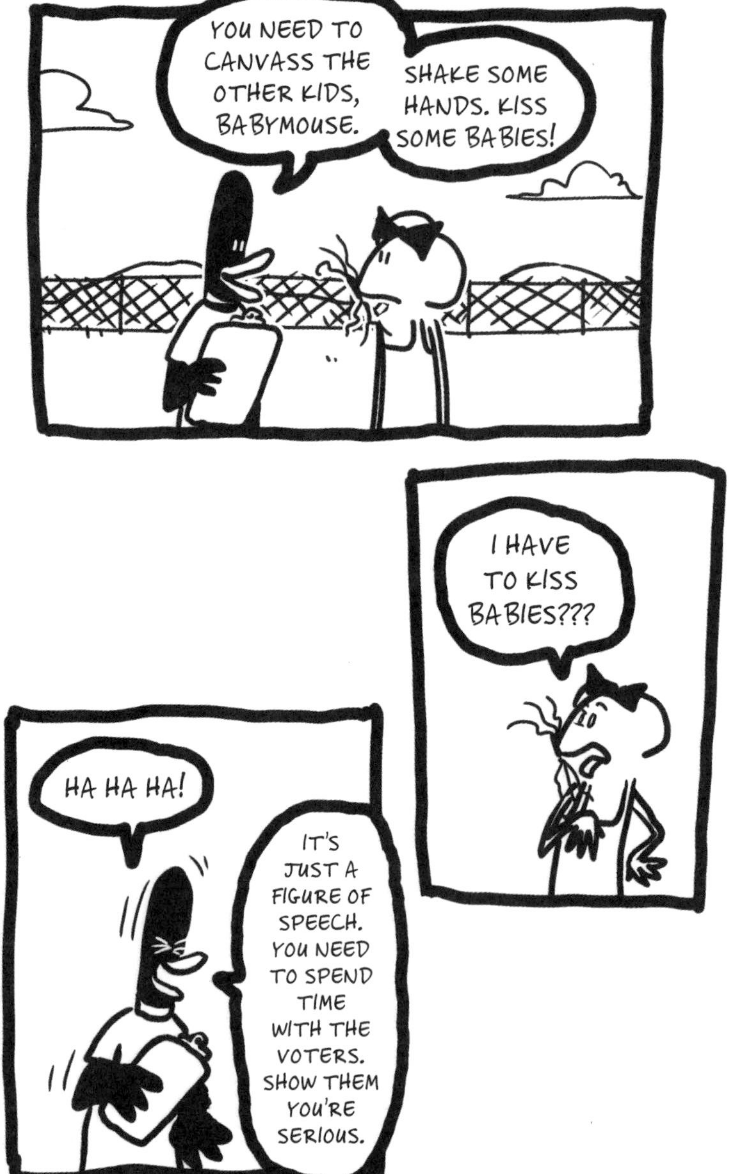
YOU NEED TO CANVASS THE OTHER KIDS, BABYMOUSE.
SHAKE SOME HANDS. KISS SOME BABIES!
I HAVE TO KISS BABIES???
HA HA HA!
IT'S JUST A FIGURE OF SPEECH. YOU NEED TO SPEND TIME WITH THE VOTERS. SHOW THEM YOU'RE SERIOUS.

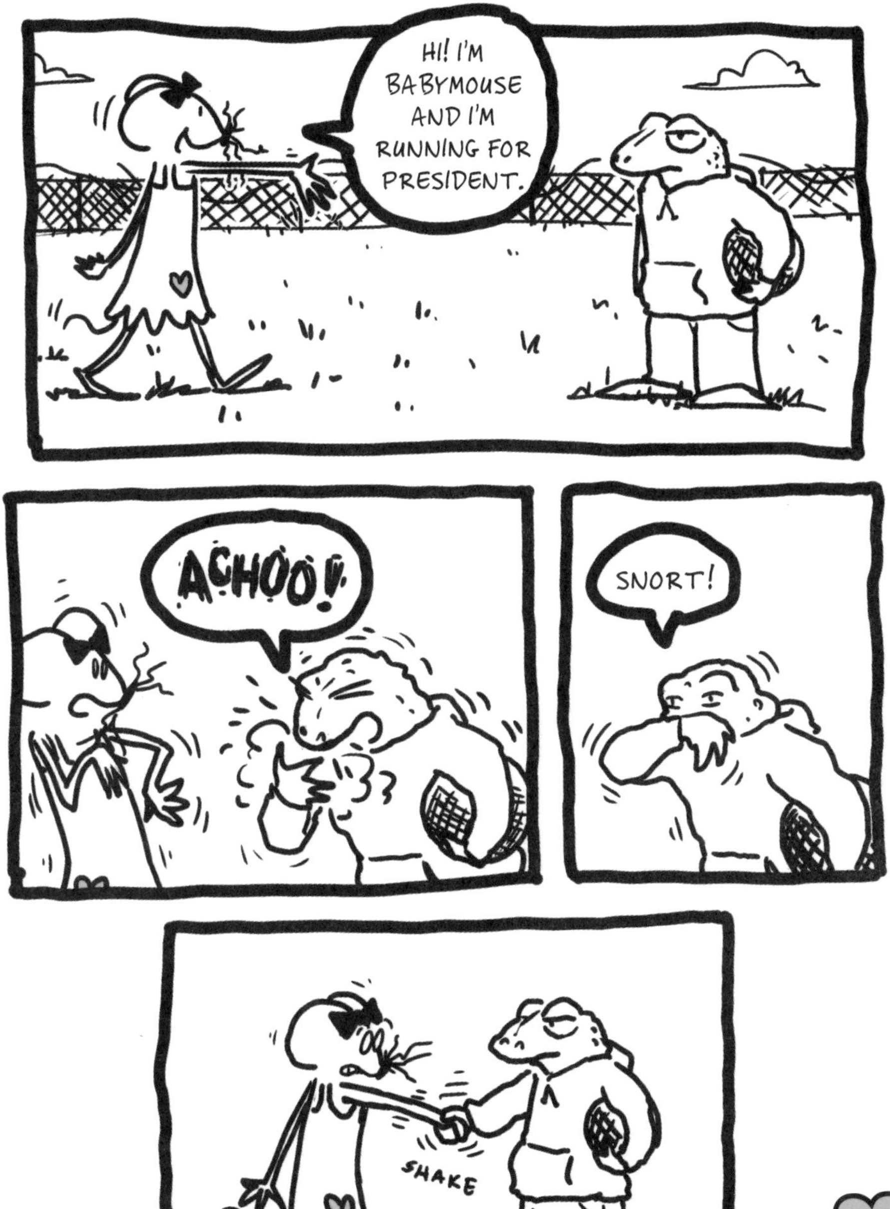
HI! I'M BABYMOUSE AND I'M RUNNING FOR PRESIDENT.
ACHOO!
SNORT!
SHAKE

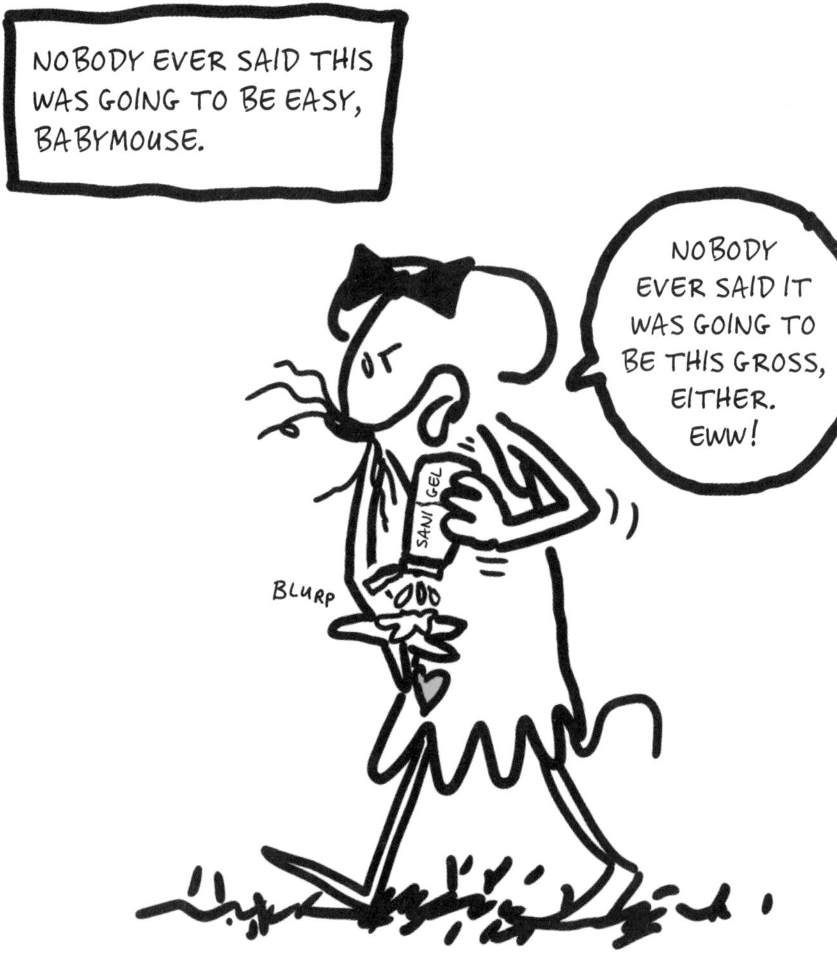
NOBODY EVER SAID THIS WAS GOING TO BE EASY, BABYMOUSE.
NOBODY EVER SAID IT WAS GOING TO BE THIS GROSS, EITHER. EWW!
SANI GEL
BLURP

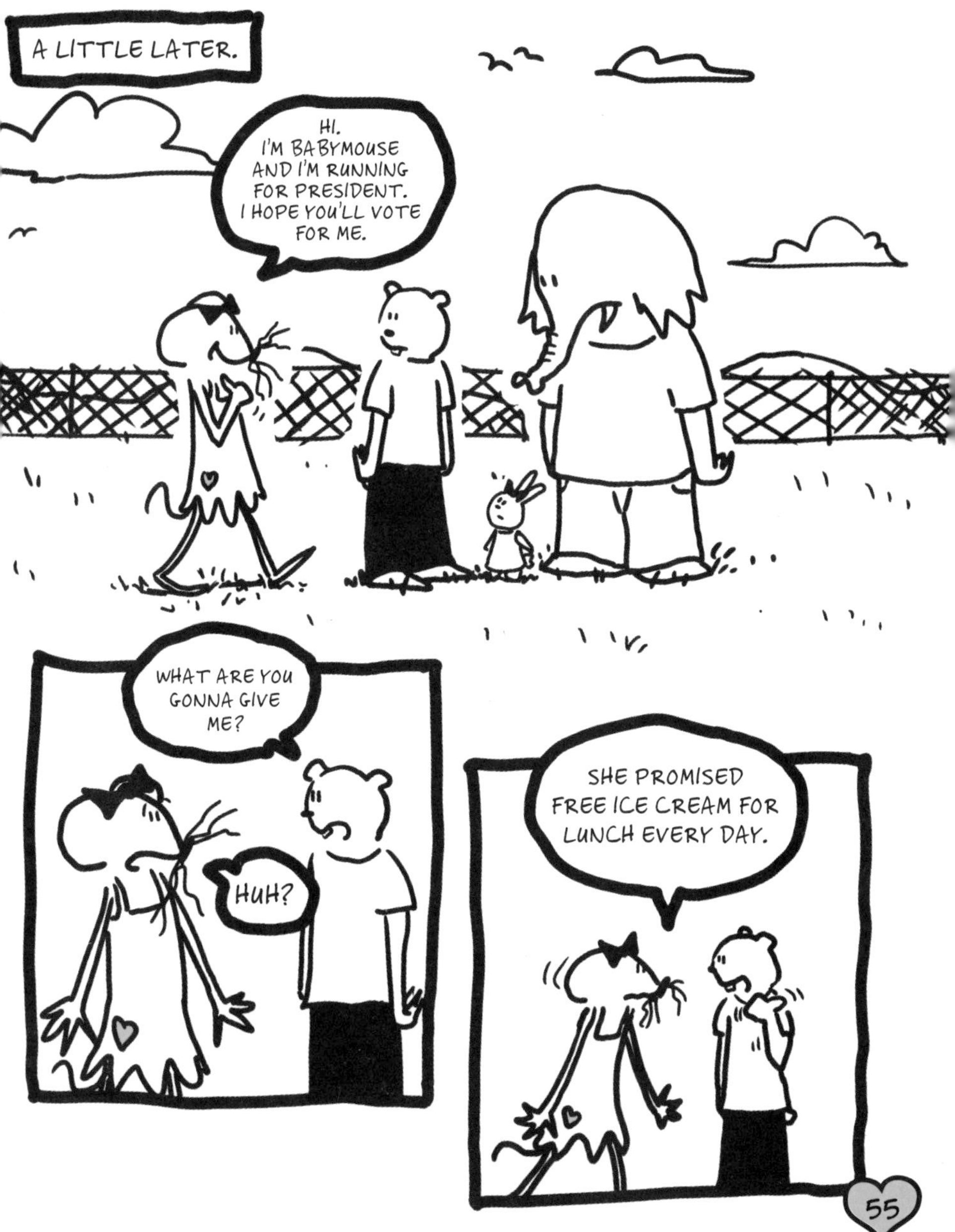
A LITTLE LATER.
HI. I'M BABYMOUSE AND I'M RUNNING FOR PRESIDENT. I HOPE YOU'LL VOTE FOR ME.
WHAT ARE YOU GONNA GIVE ME?
HUH?
SHE PROMISED FREE ICE CREAM FOR LUNCH EVERY DAY.

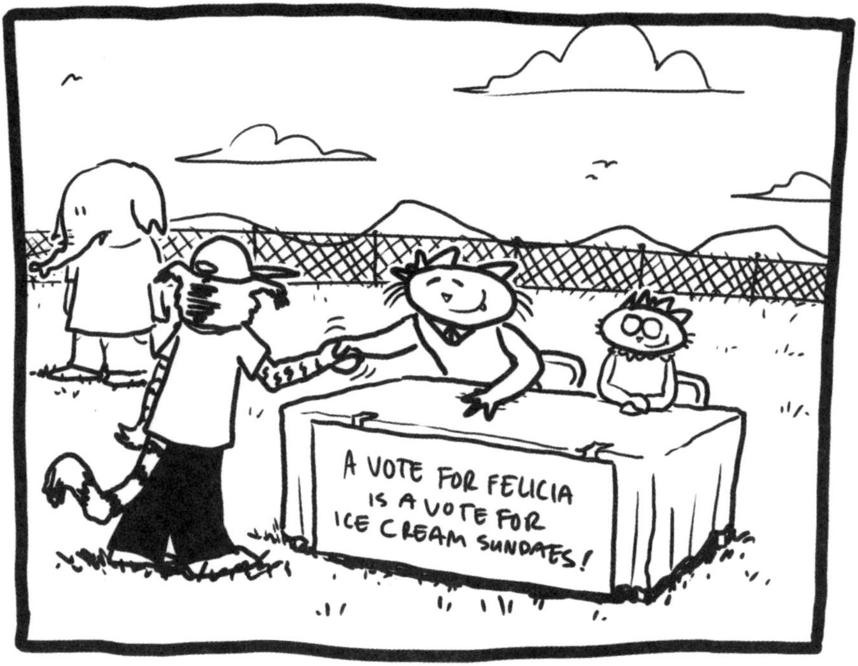
A VOTE FOR FELICIA IS A VOTE FOR ICE CREAM SUNDAES!

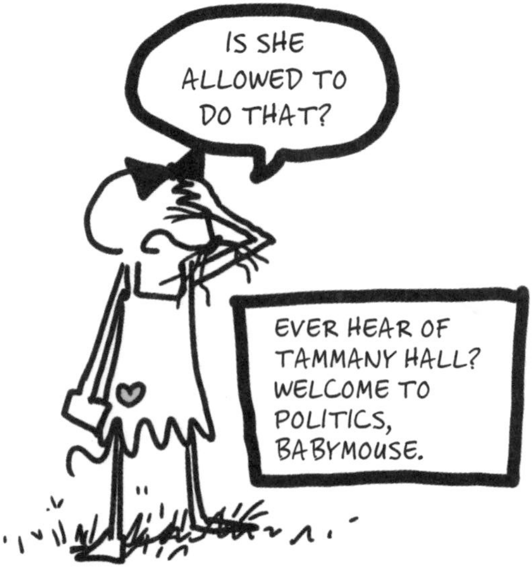
IS SHE ALLOWED TO DO THAT?
EVER HEAR OF TAMMANY HALL? WELCOME TO POLITICS, BABYMOUSE.

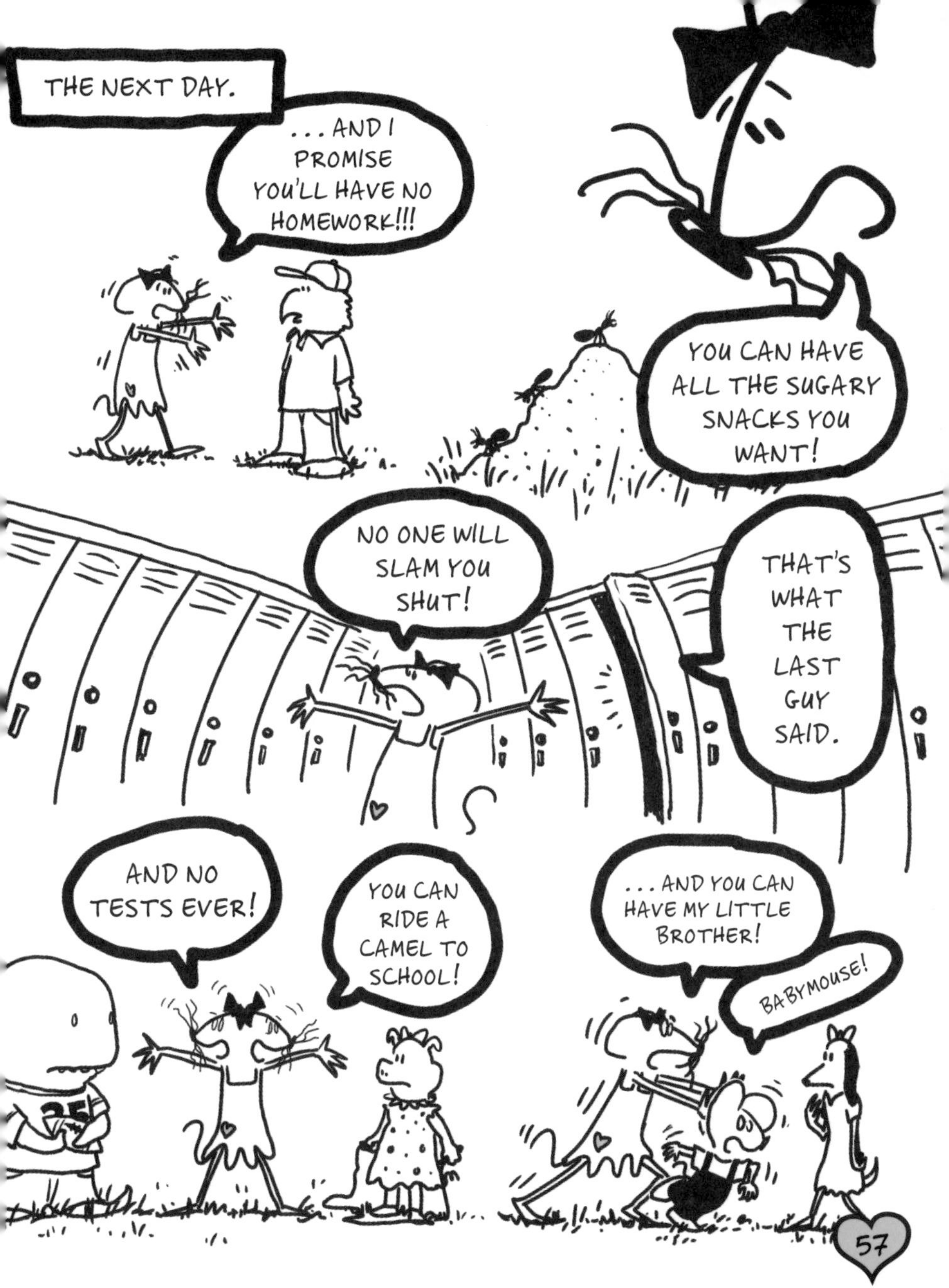
THE NEXT DAY.
...AND I PROMISE YOU'LL HAVE NO HOMEWORK!!!
YOU CAN HAVE ALL THE SUGARY SNACKS YOU WANT!
NO ONE WILL SLAM YOU SHUT!
THAT'S WHAT THE LAST GUY SAID.
AND NO TESTS EVER!
YOU CAN RIDE A CAMEL TO SCHOOL!
...AND YOU CAN HAVE MY LITTLE BROTHER!
BABYMOUSE!
25

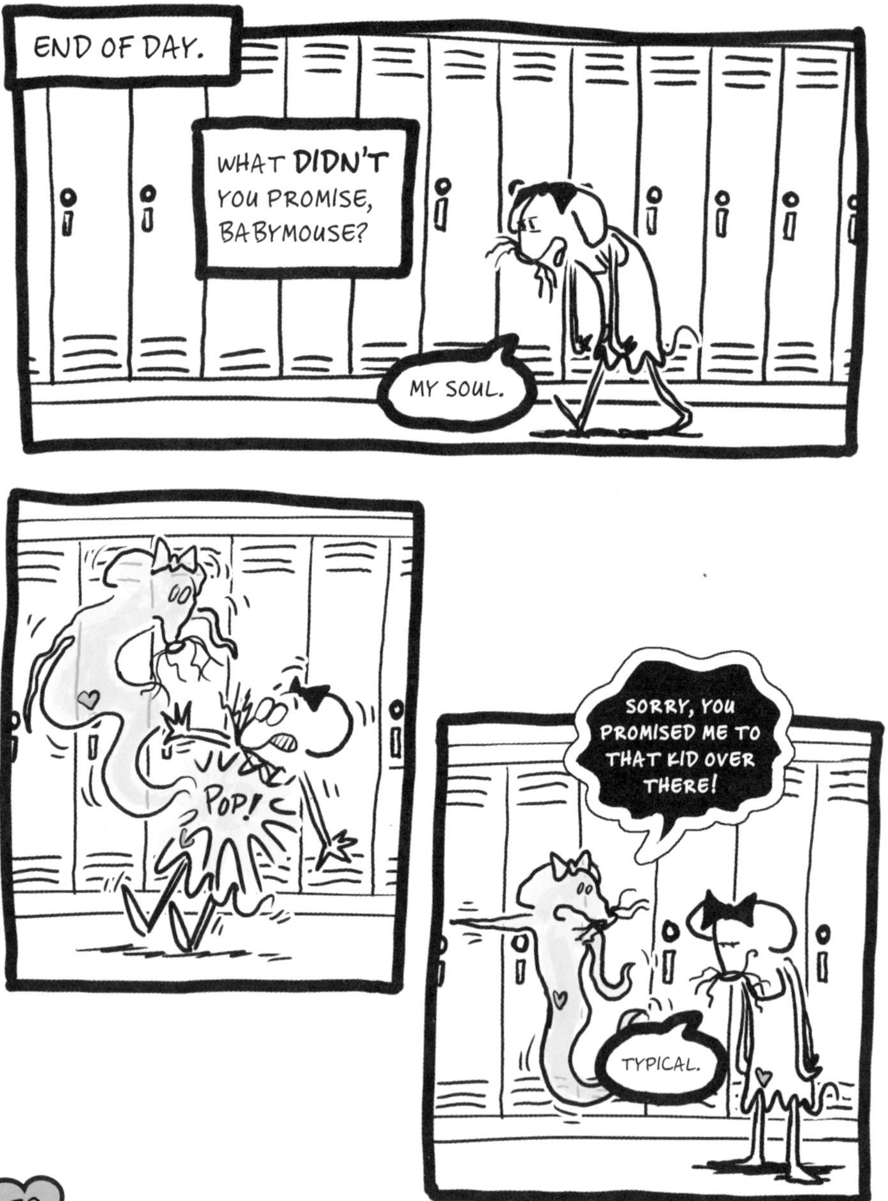
END OF DAY.
WHAT DIDN'T YOU PROMISE, BABYMOUSE?
MY SOUL.
POP!
SORRY, YOU PROMISED ME TO THAT KID OVER THERE!
TYPICAL.

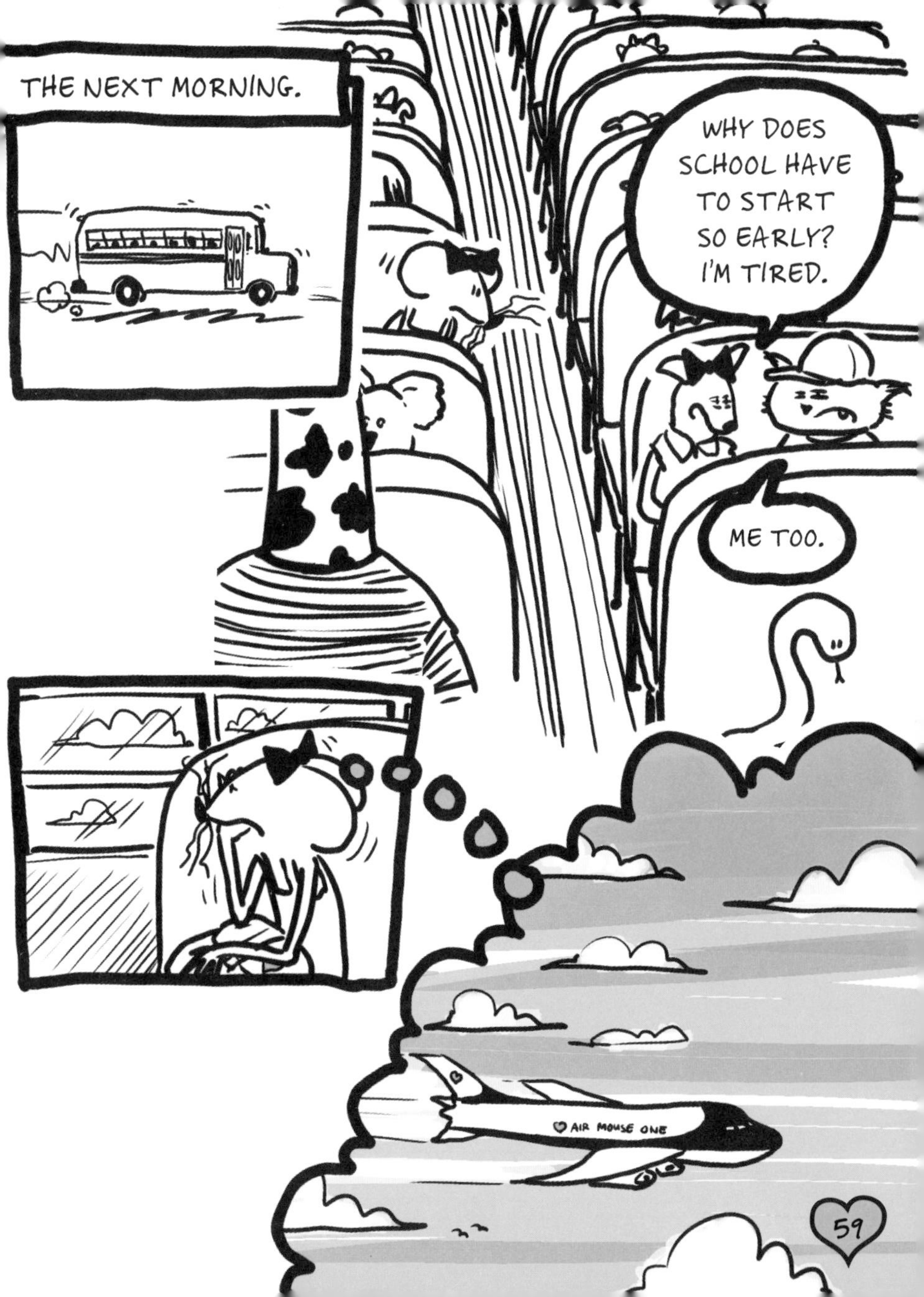
THE NEXT MORNING.
WHY DOES SCHOOL HAVE TO START SO EARLY? I'M TIRED.
ME TOO.
AIR MOUSE ONE

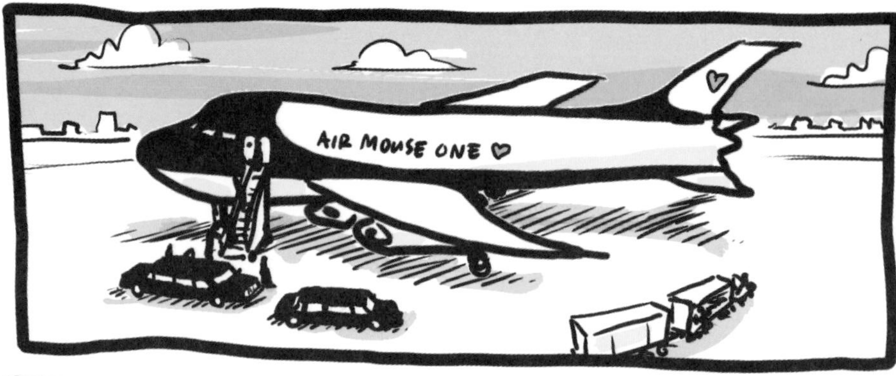
AIR MOUSE ONE

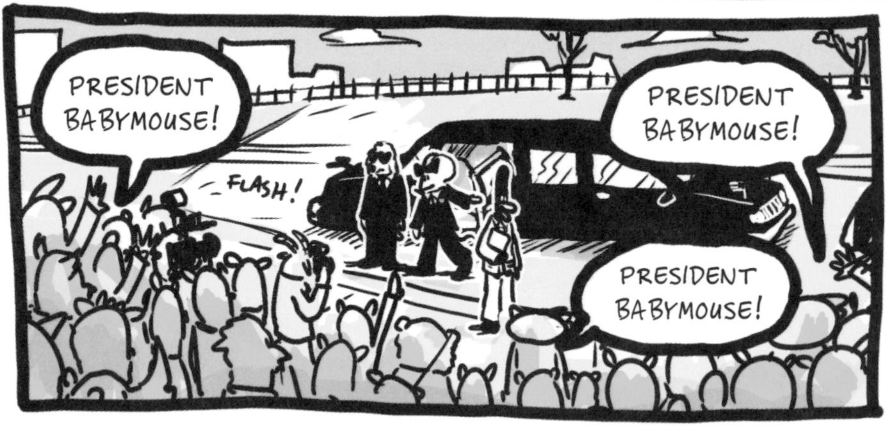
PRESIDENT BABYMOUSE!
FLASH!
PRESIDENT BABYMOUSE!
PRESIDENT BABYMOUSE!

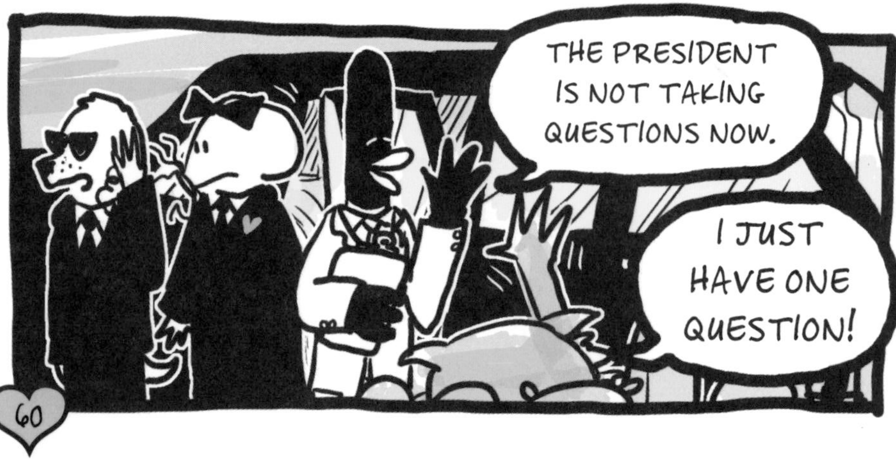
THE PRESIDENT IS NOT TAKING QUESTIONS NOW.
I JUST HAVE ONE QUESTION!

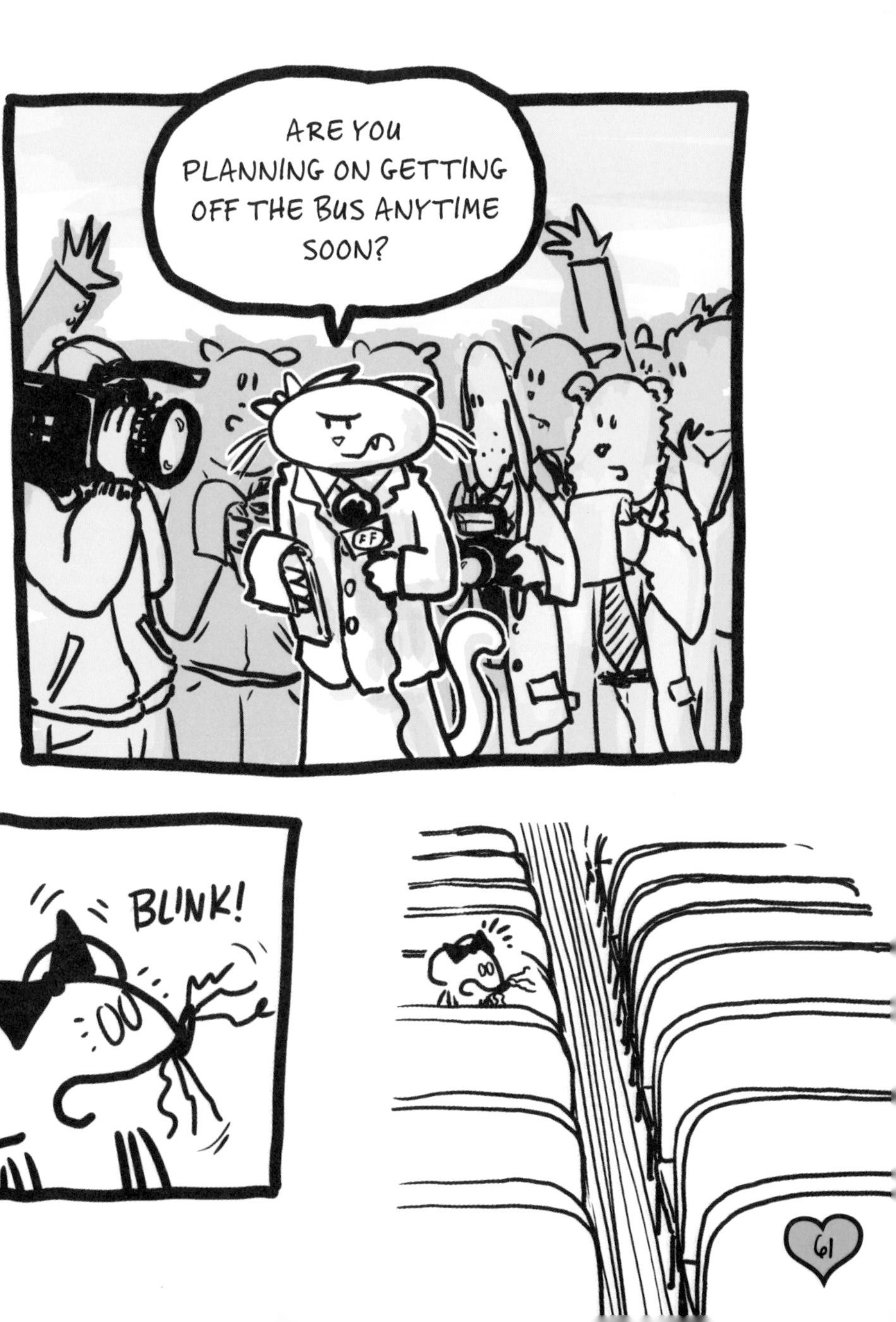
ARE YOU PLANNING ON GETTING OFF THE BUS ANYTIME SOON?
FF
BLINK!

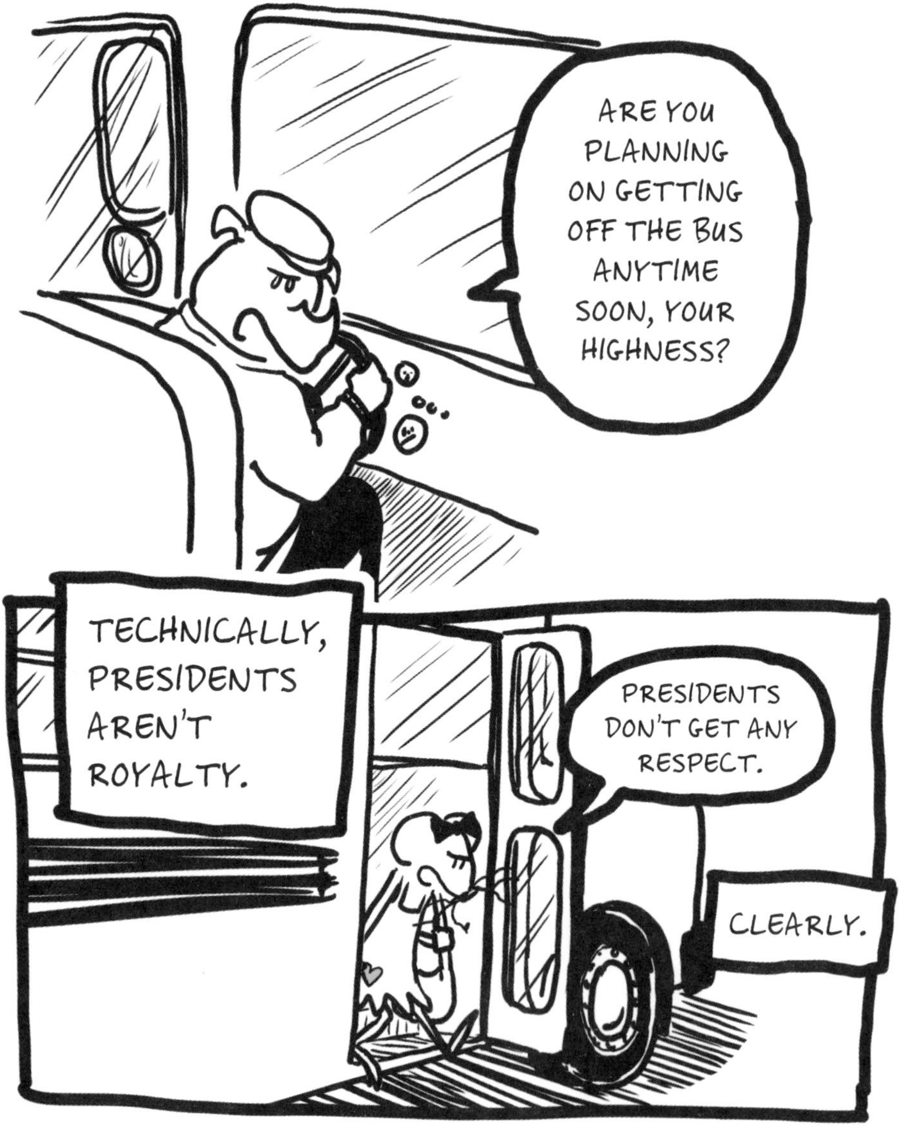
ARE YOU PLANNING ON GETTING OFF THE BUS ANYTIME SOON, YOUR HIGHNESS?
TECHNICALLY, PRESIDENTS AREN'T ROYALTY.
PRESIDENTS DON'T GET ANY RESPECT.
CLEARLY.

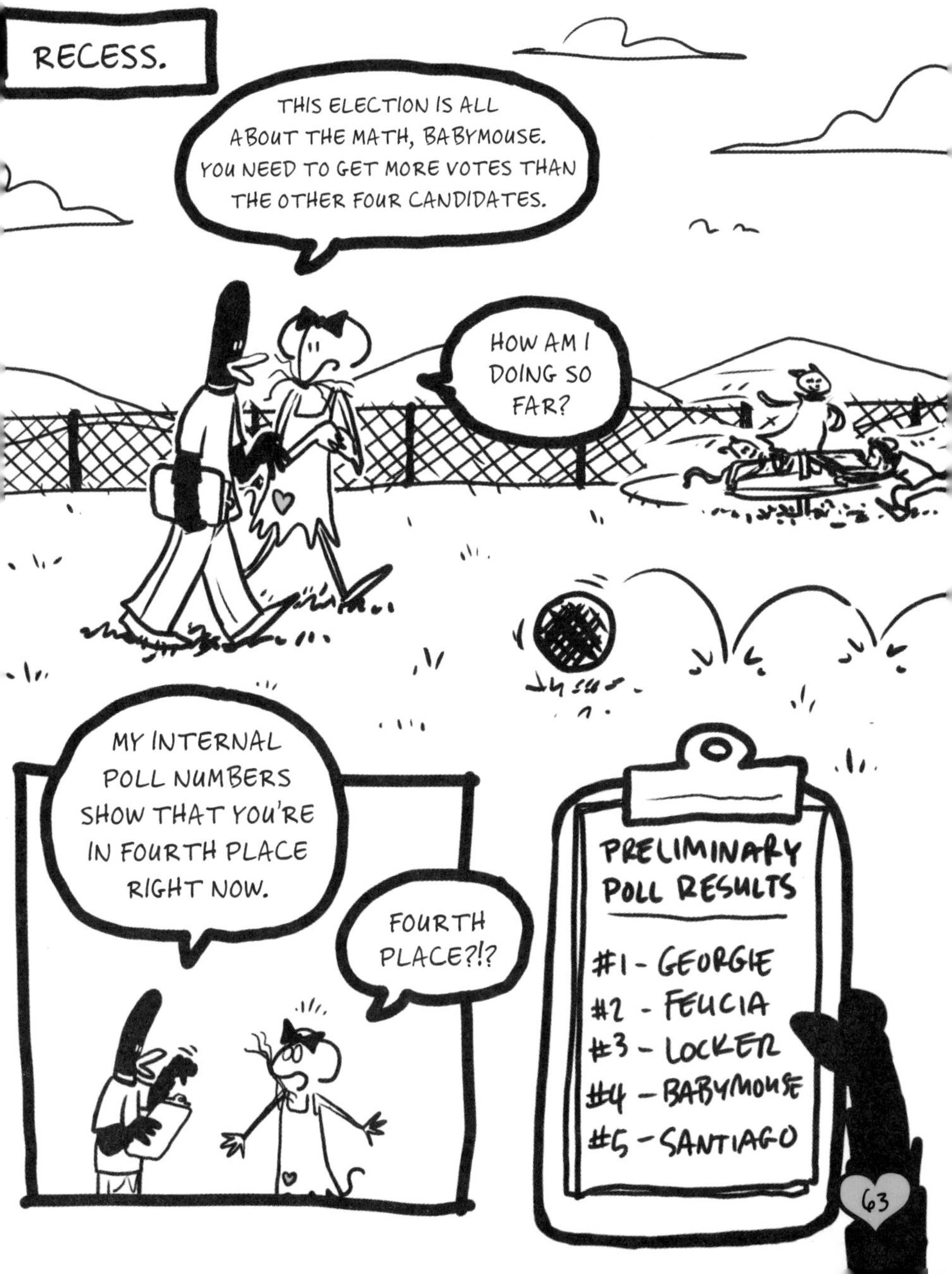
RECESS.
THIS ELECTION IS ALL ABOUT THE MATH, BABYMOUSE. YOU NEED TO GET MORE VOTES THAN THE OTHER FOUR CANDIDATES.
HOW AM I DOING SO FAR?
MY INTERNAL POLL NUMBERS SHOW THAT YOU'RE IN FOURTH PLACE RIGHT NOW.
FOURTH PLACE?!?
PRELIMINARY POLL RESULTS
#1 - GEORGIE
#2 - FELICIA
#3 - LOCKER
#4 - BABYMOUSE
#5 - SANTIAGO

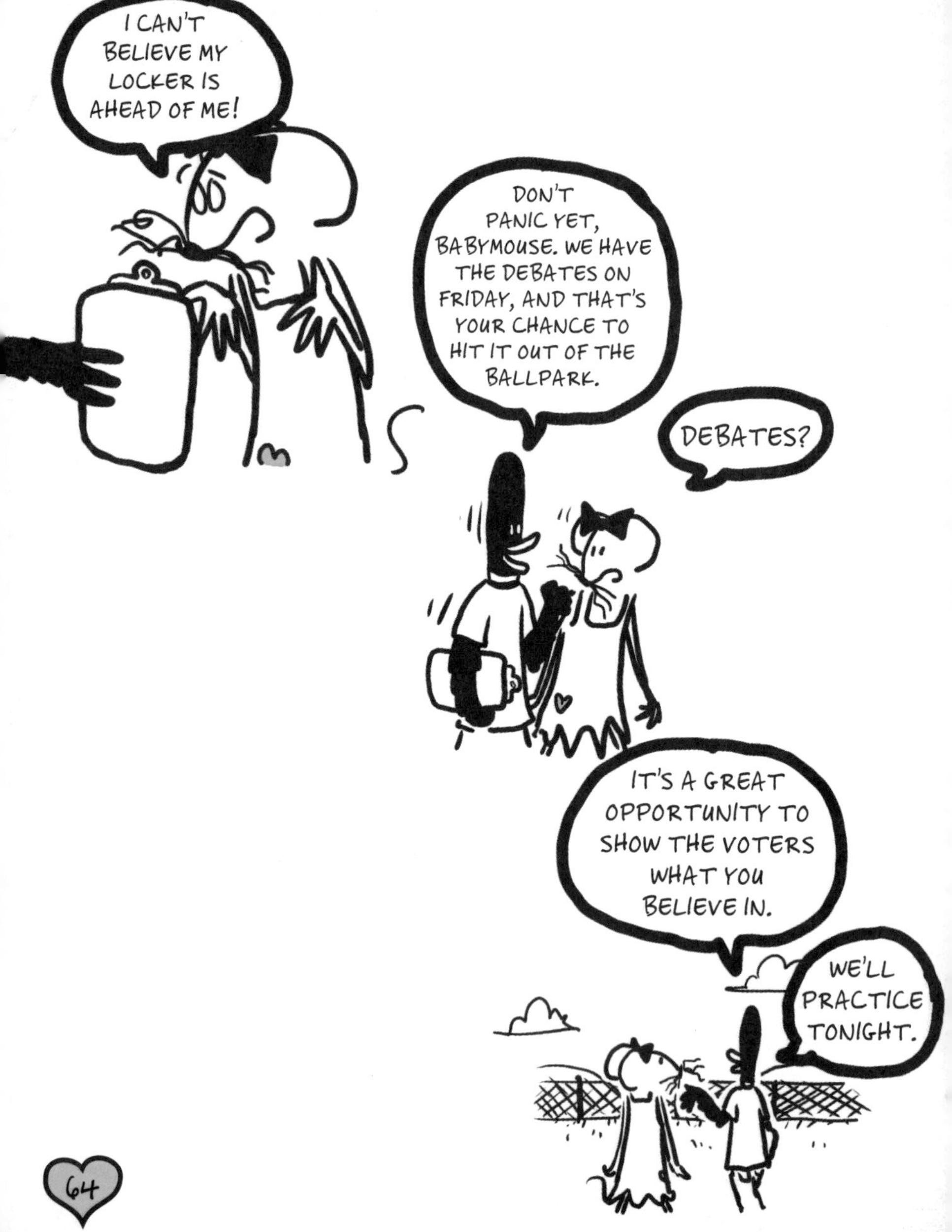
I CAN'T BELIEVE MY LOCKER IS AHEAD OF ME!
DON'T PANIC YET, BABYMOUSE. WE HAVE THE DEBATES ON FRIDAY, AND THAT'S YOUR CHANCE TO HIT IT OUT OF THE BALLPARK.
DEBATES?
IT'S A GREAT OPPORTUNITY TO SHOW THE VOTERS WHAT YOU BELIEVE IN.
WE'LL PRACTICE TONIGHT.

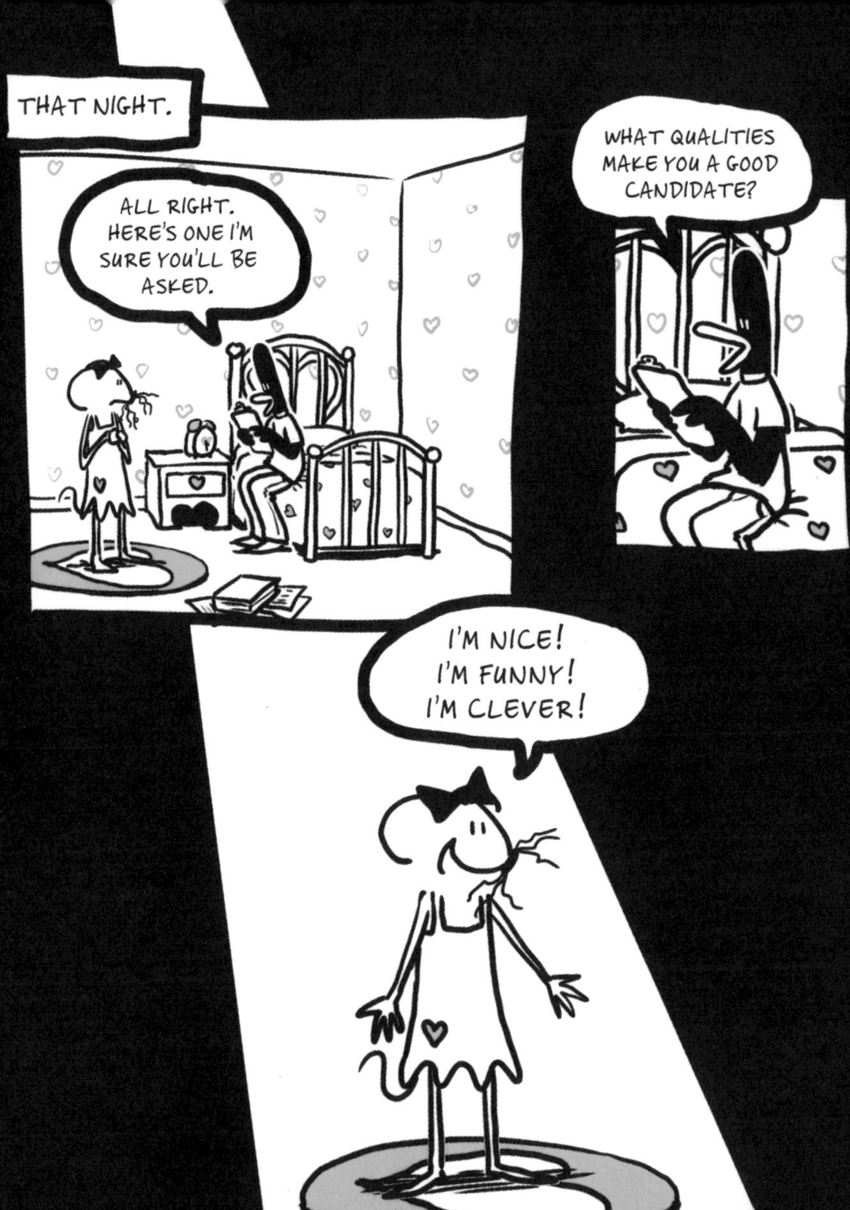
THAT NIGHT.
ALL RIGHT. HERE'S ONE I'M SURE YOU'LL BE ASKED.
WHAT QUALITIES MAKE YOU A GOOD CANDIDATE?
I'M NICE! I'M FUNNY! I'M CLEVER!

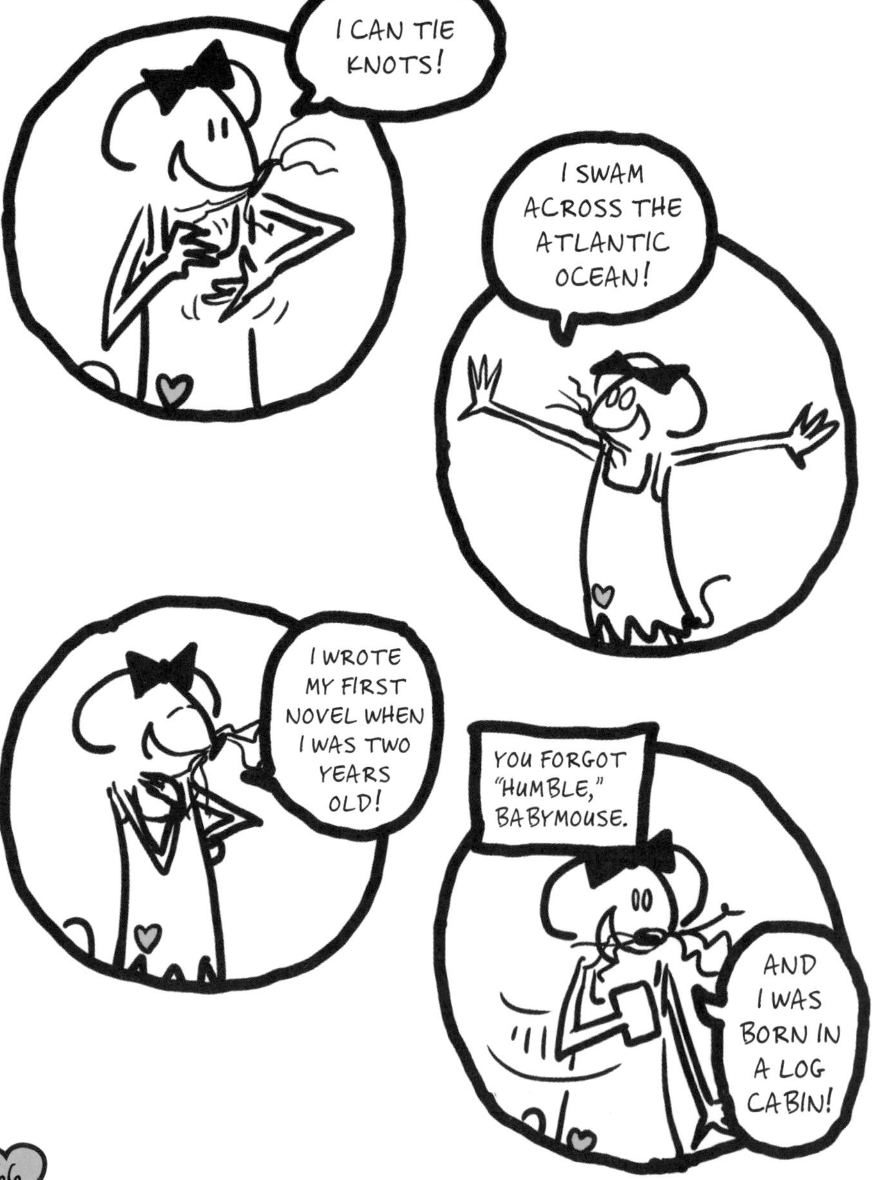
I CAN TIE KNOTS!
I SWAM ACROSS THE ATLANTIC OCEAN!
I WROTE MY FIRST NOVEL WHEN I WAS TWO YEARS OLD!
YOU FORGOT "HUMBLE," BABYMOUSE.
AND I WAS BORN IN A LOG CABIN!

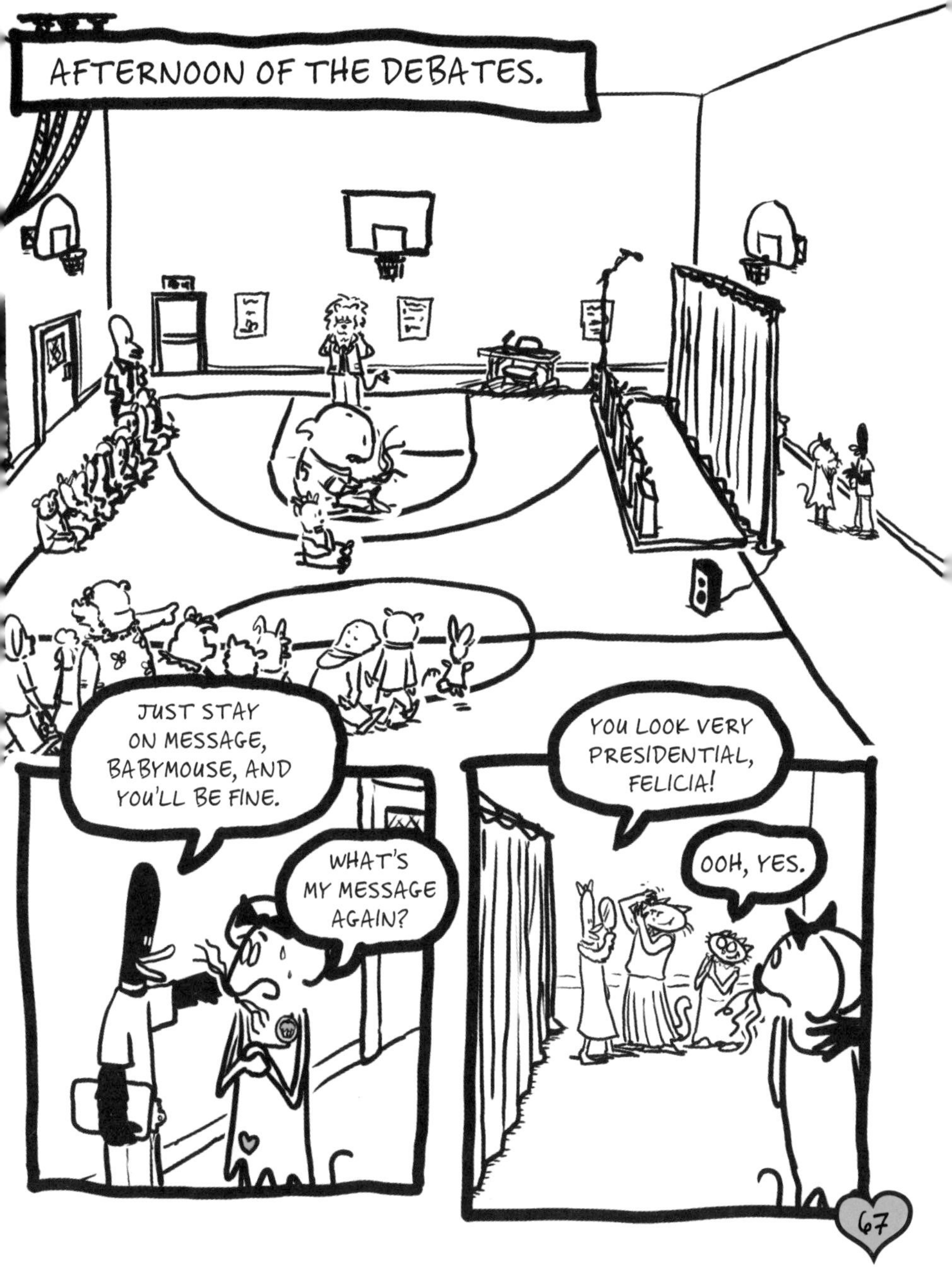
AFTERNOON OF THE DEBATES.
JUST STAY ON MESSAGE, BABYMOUSE, AND YOU'LL BE FINE.
WHAT'S MY MESSAGE AGAIN?
YOU LOOK VERY PRESIDENTIAL, FELICIA!
OOH, YES.

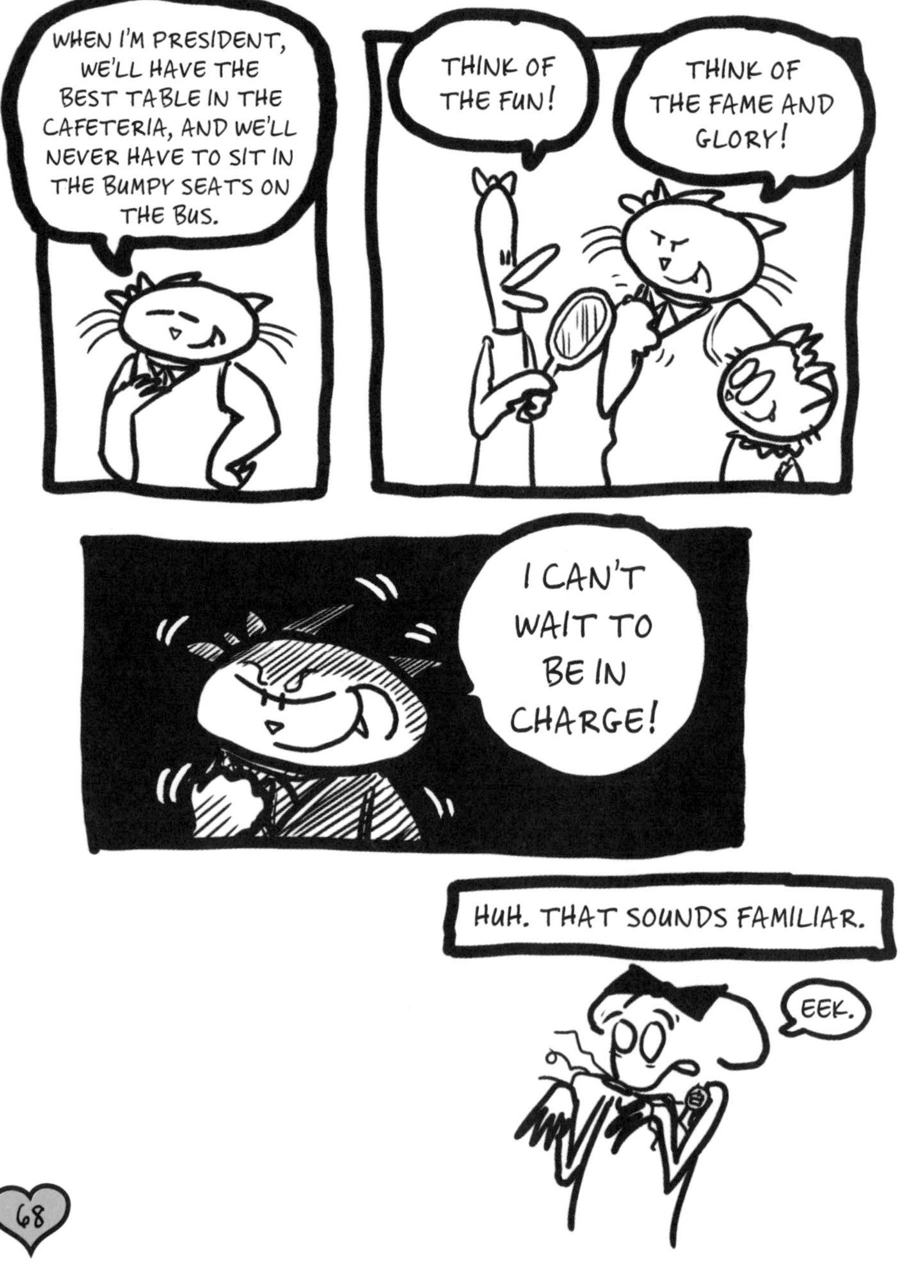
WHEN I'M PRESIDENT, WE'LL HAVE THE BEST TABLE IN THE CAFETERIA, AND WE'LL NEVER HAVE TO SIT IN THE BUMPY SEATS ON THE BUS.
THINK OF THE FUN!
THINK OF THE FAME AND GLORY!
I CAN'T WAIT TO BE IN CHARGE!
HUH. THAT SOUNDS FAMILIAR.
EEK.

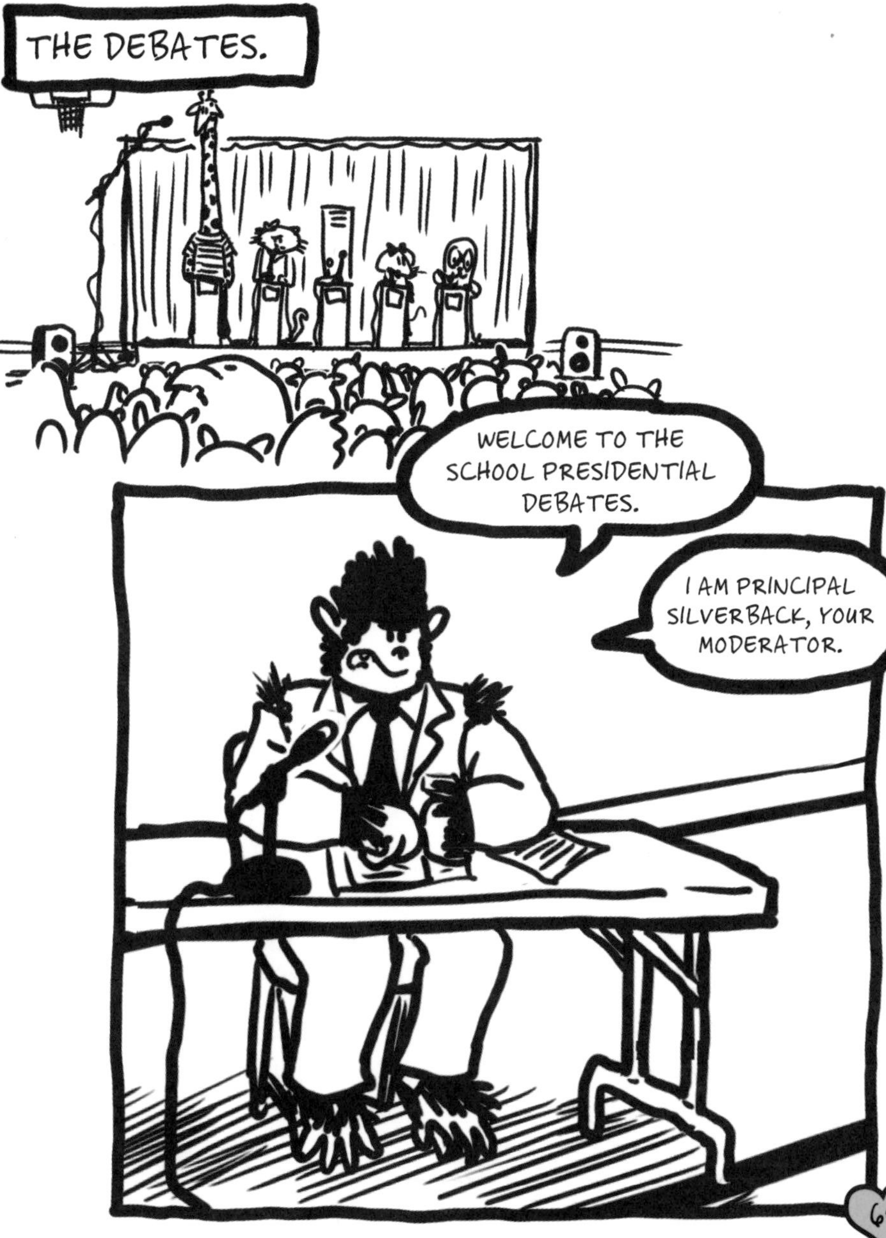
THE DEBATES.
WELCOME TO THE SCHOOL PRESIDENTIAL DEBATES.
I AM PRINCIPAL SILVERBACK, YOUR MODERATOR.

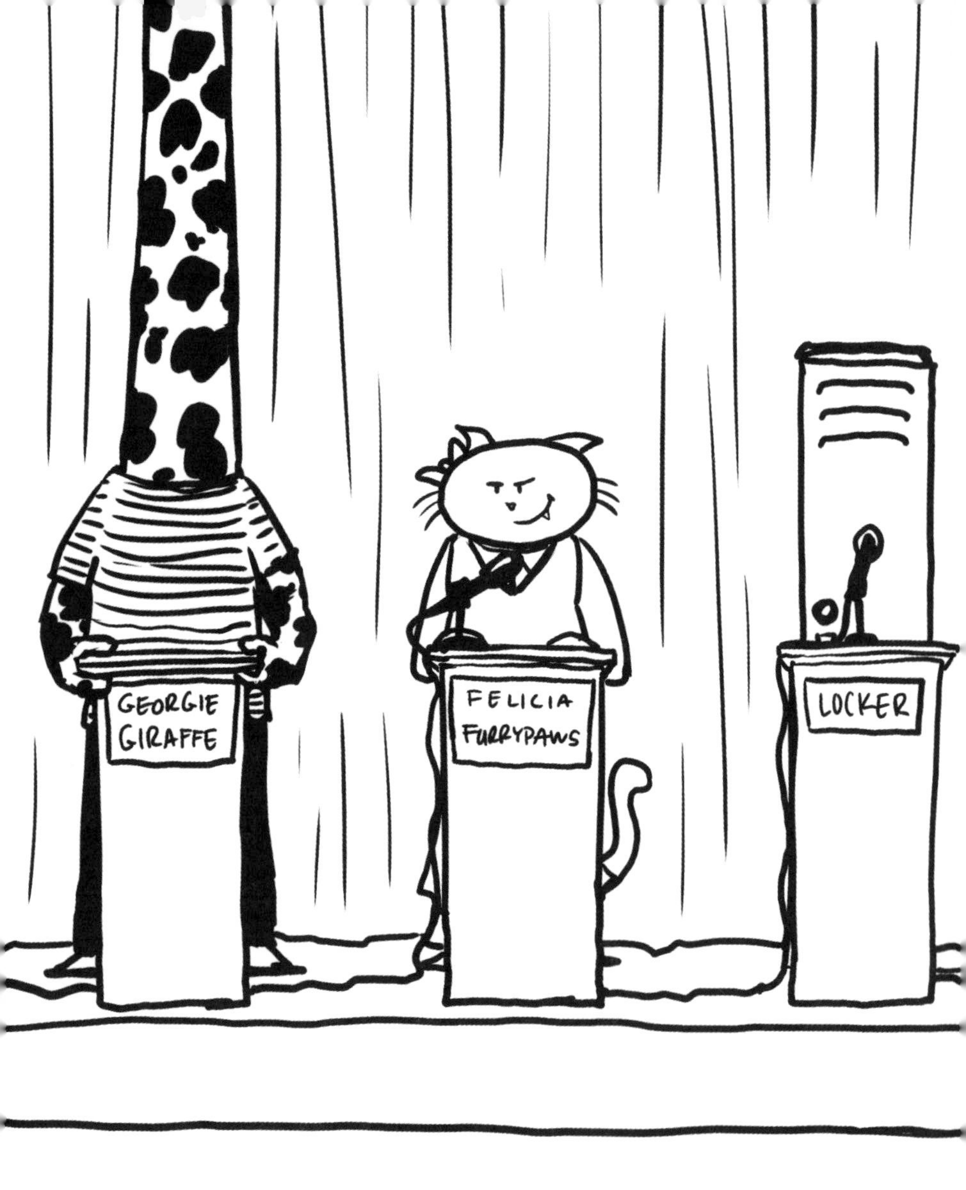
GEORGIE GIRAFFE
FELICIA FURRYPAWS
LOCKER

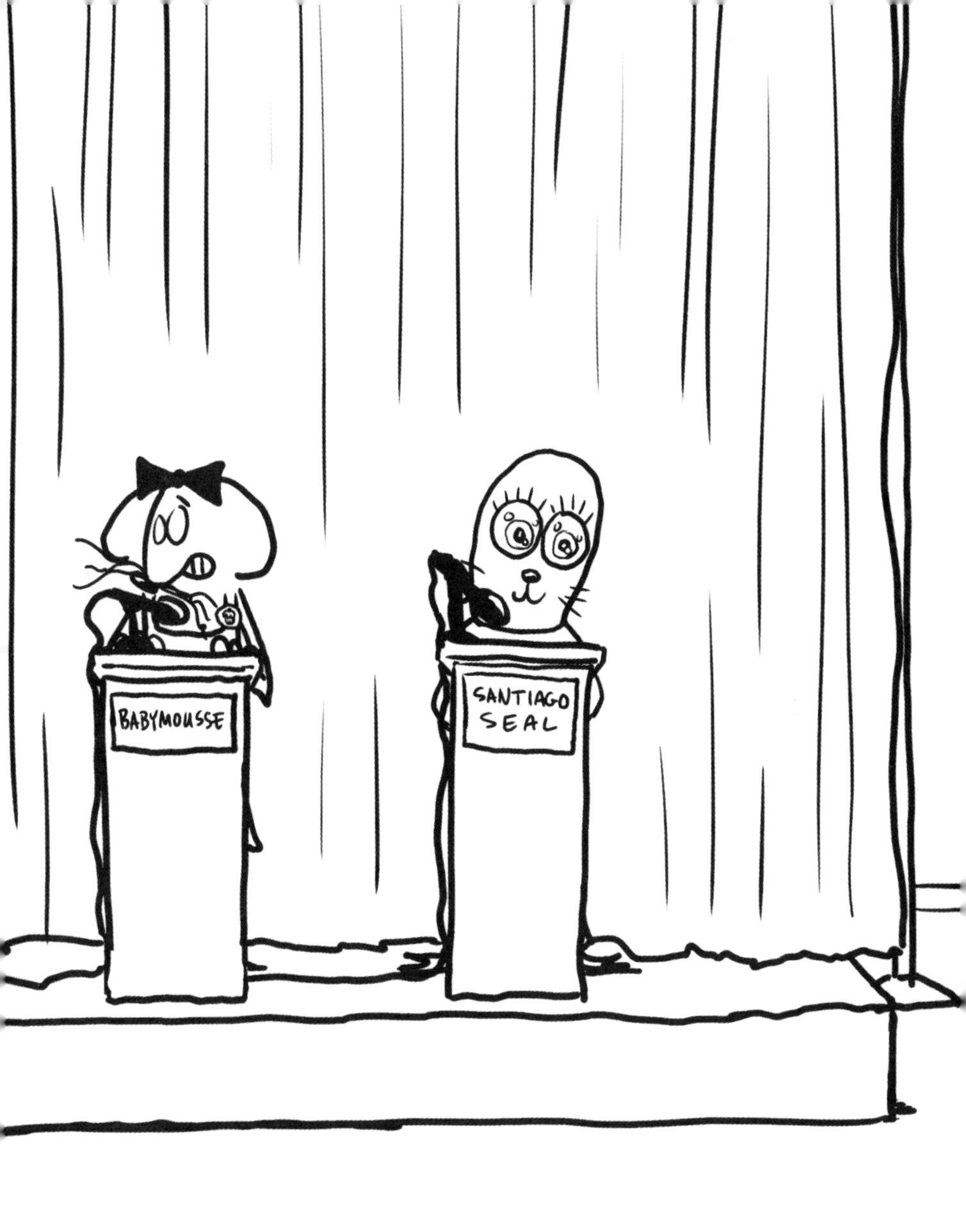
BABYMOUSSE
SANTIAGO SEAL

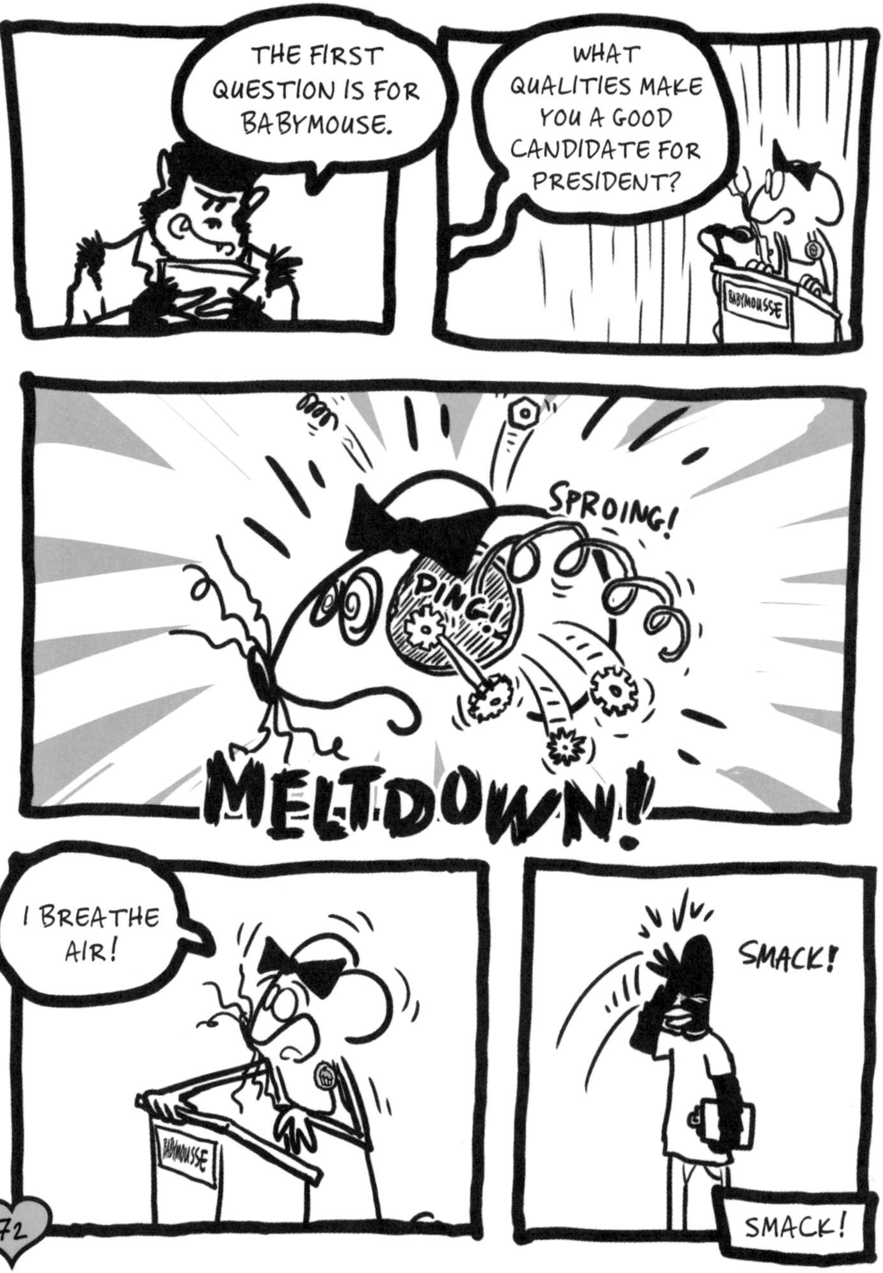

THE FIRST QUESTION IS FOR BABYMOUSE.
WHAT QUALITIES MAKE YOU A GOOD CANDIDATE FOR PRESIDENT?
BABYMOUSSE
SPROING!
PING!
MELTDOWN!
I BREATHE AIR!
BABYMOUSSE
SMACK!
SMACK!

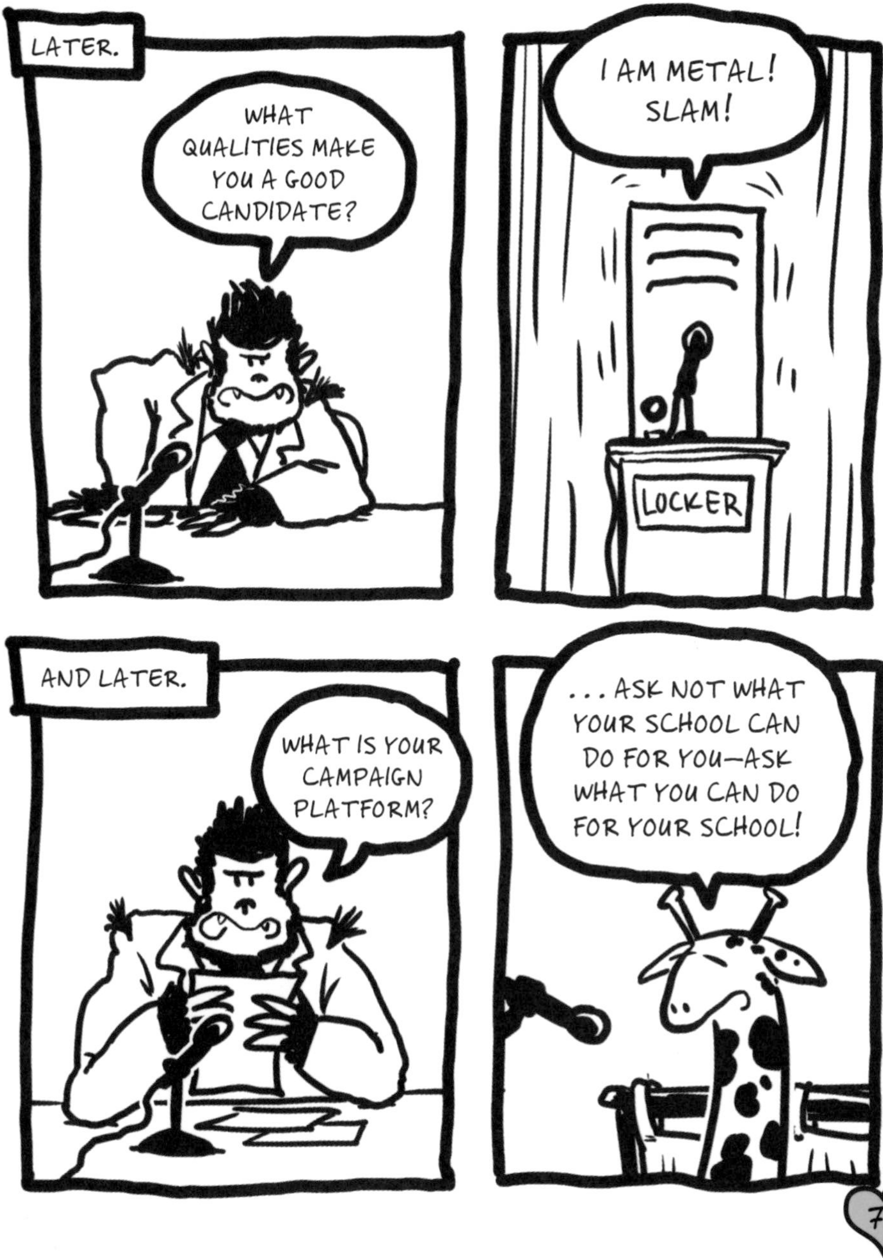
LATER.
WHAT QUALITIES MAKE YOU A GOOD CANDIDATE?
I AM METAL! SLAM!
LOCKER
AND LATER.
WHAT IS YOUR CAMPAIGN PLATFORM?
...ASK NOT WHAT YOUR SCHOOL CAN DO FOR YOU—ASK WHAT YOU CAN DO FOR YOUR SCHOOL!

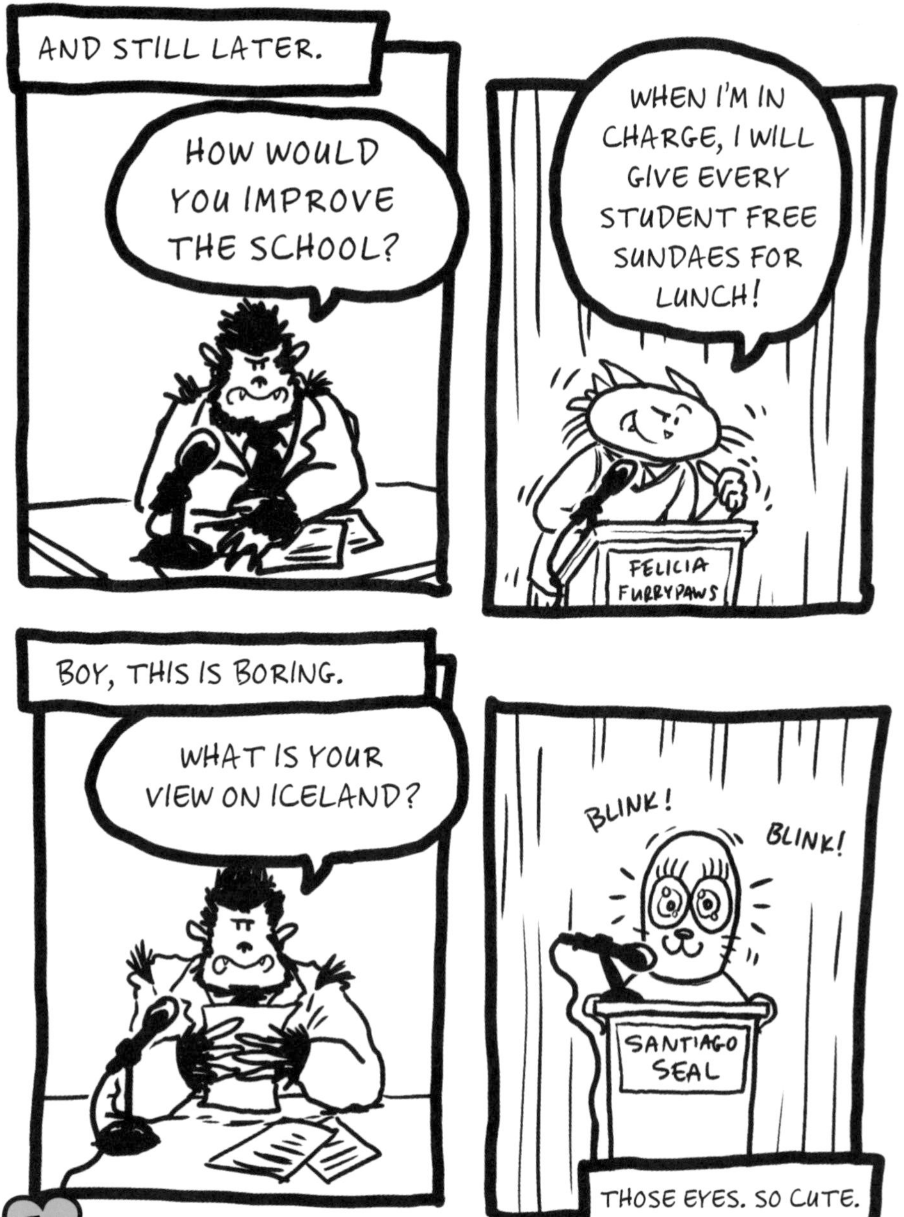
AND STILL LATER.
HOW WOULD YOU IMPROVE THE SCHOOL?
WHEN I'M IN CHARGE, I WILL GIVE EVERY STUDENT FREE SUNDAES FOR LUNCH!
FELICIA FURRYPAWS
BOY, THIS IS BORING.
WHAT IS YOUR VIEW ON ICELAND?
BLINK!
BLINK!
SANTIAGO SEAL
THOSE EYES. SO CUTE.

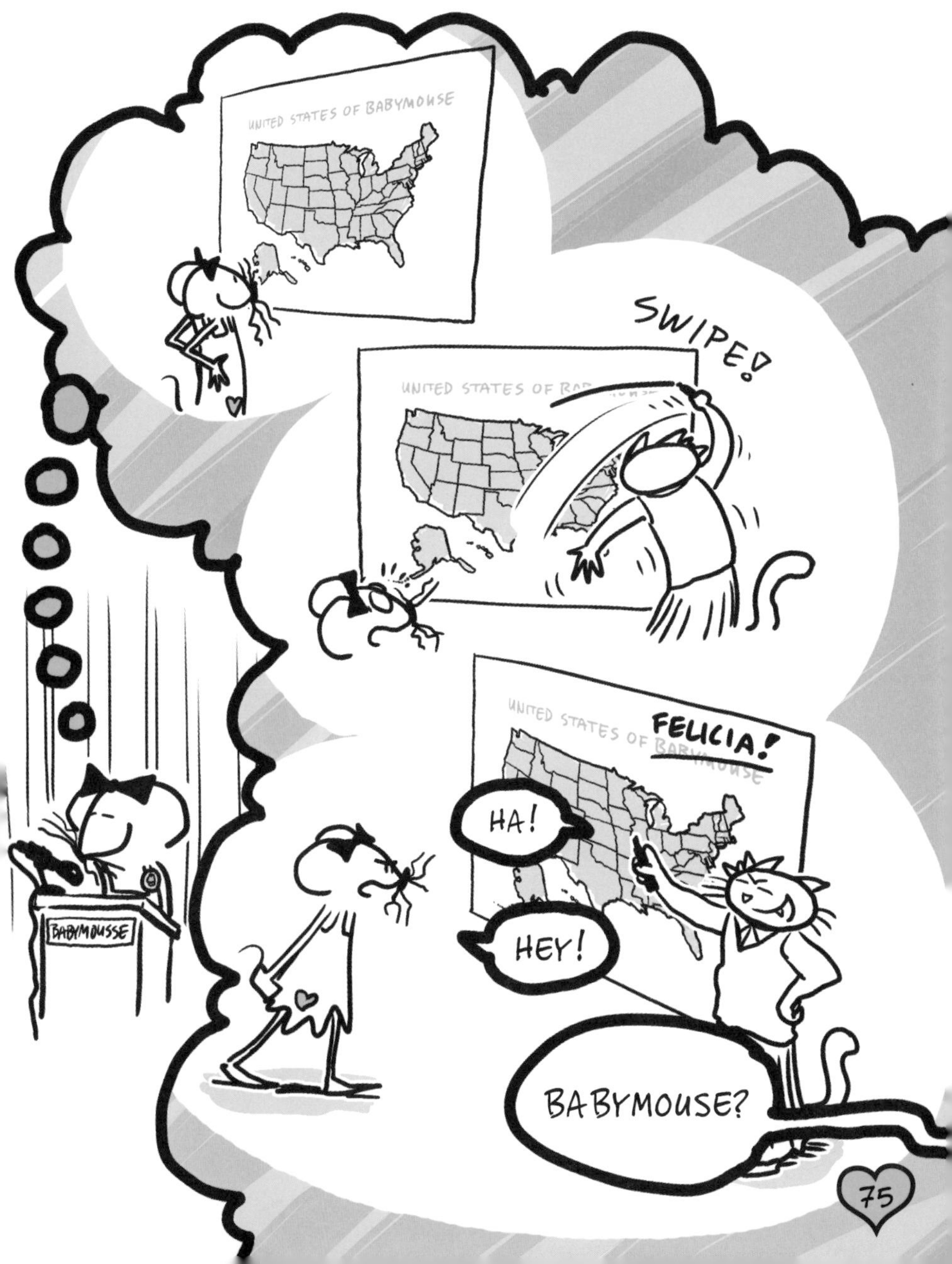
UNITED STATES OF BABYMOUSE
SWIPE!
UNITED STATES OF BABYMOUSE
UNITED STATES OF BABYMOUSE
FELICIA!
HA!
HEY!
BABYMOUSSE
BABYMOUSE?

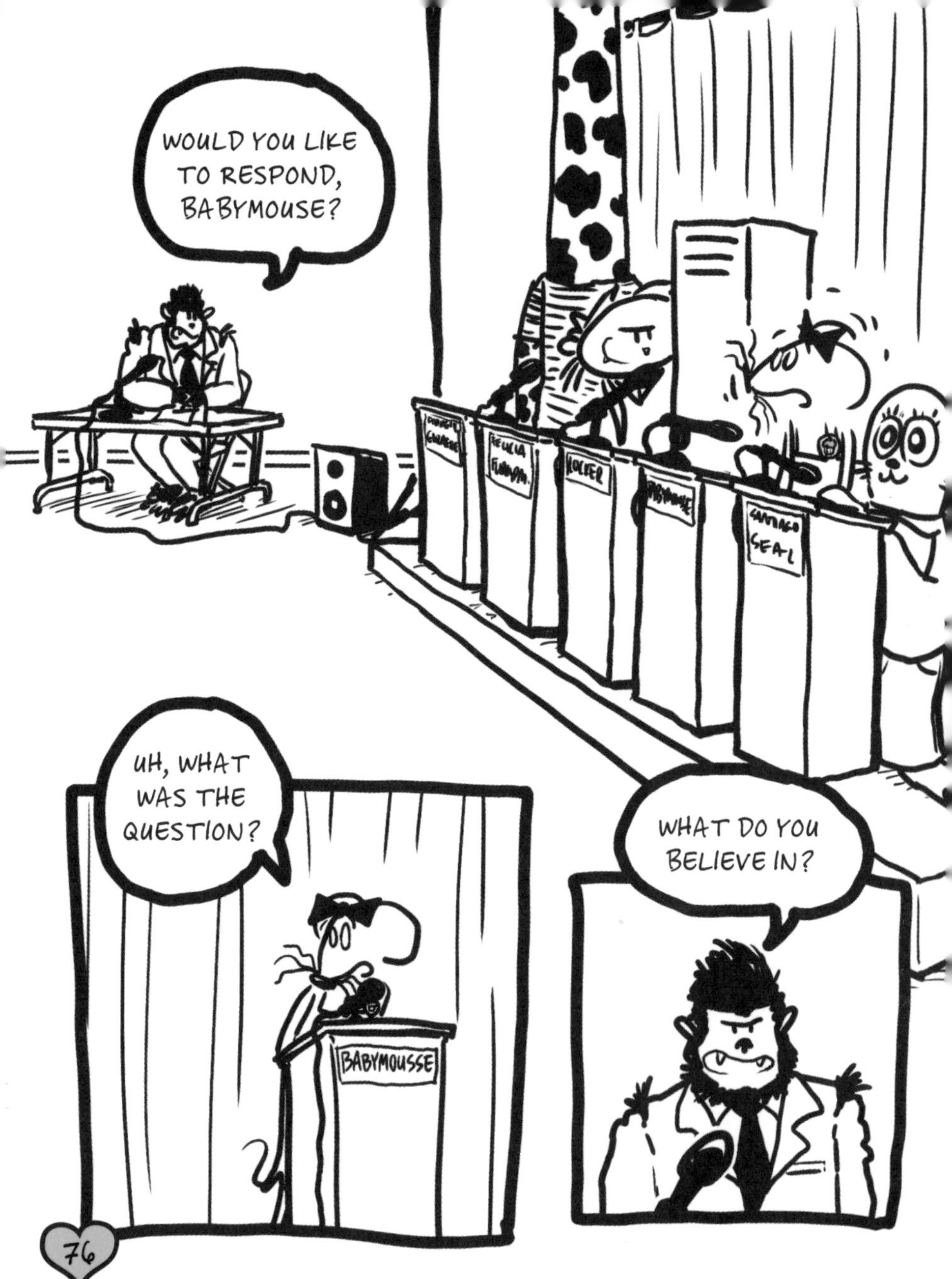
WOULD YOU LIKE TO RESPOND, BABYMOUSE?
LOCKER
SANTIAGO SEAL
UH, WHAT WAS THE QUESTION?
BABYMOUSSE
WHAT DO YOU BELIEVE IN?

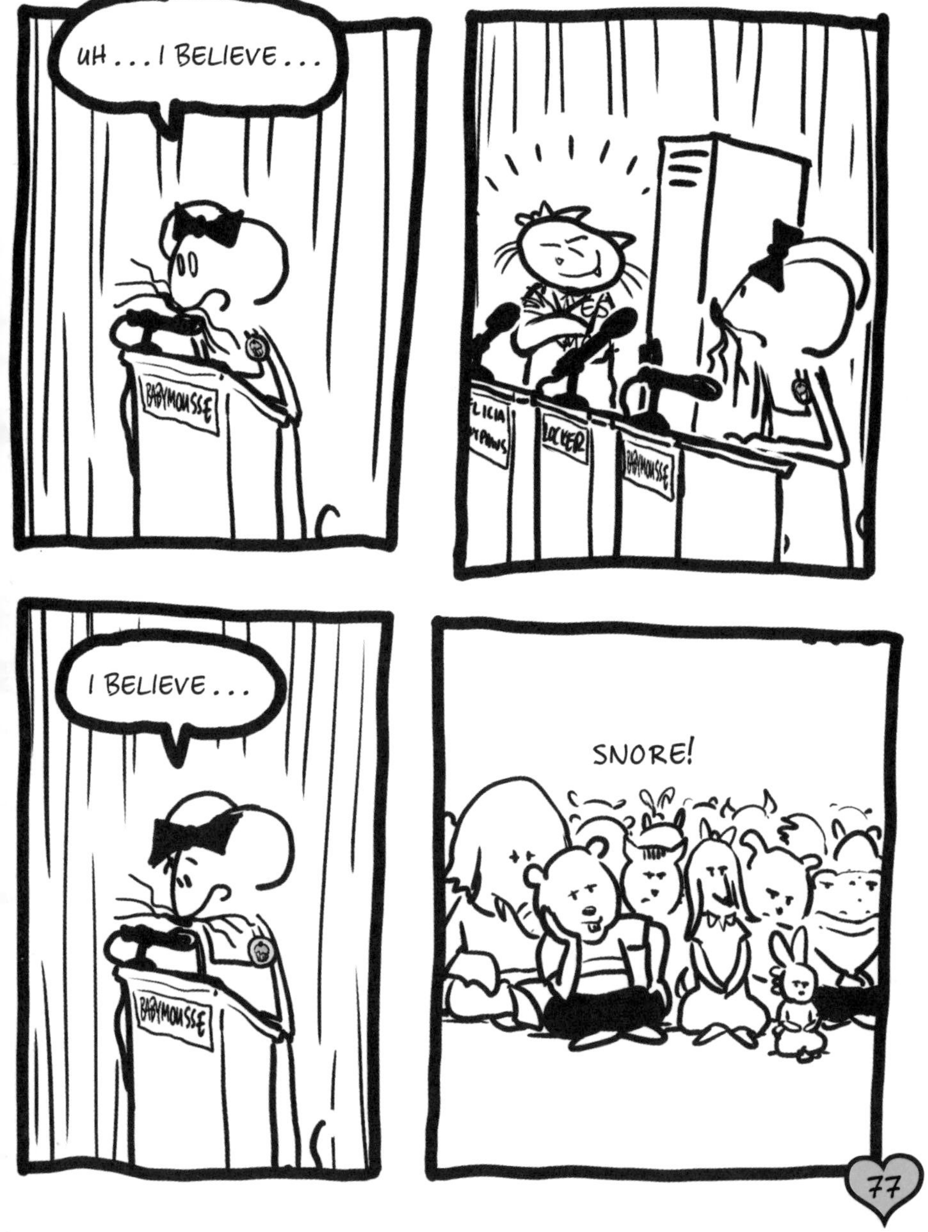
UH . . . I BELIEVE . . .
BABYMOUSSE
LOCKER
BABYMOUSSE
I BELIEVE . . .
BABYMOUSSE
SNORE!

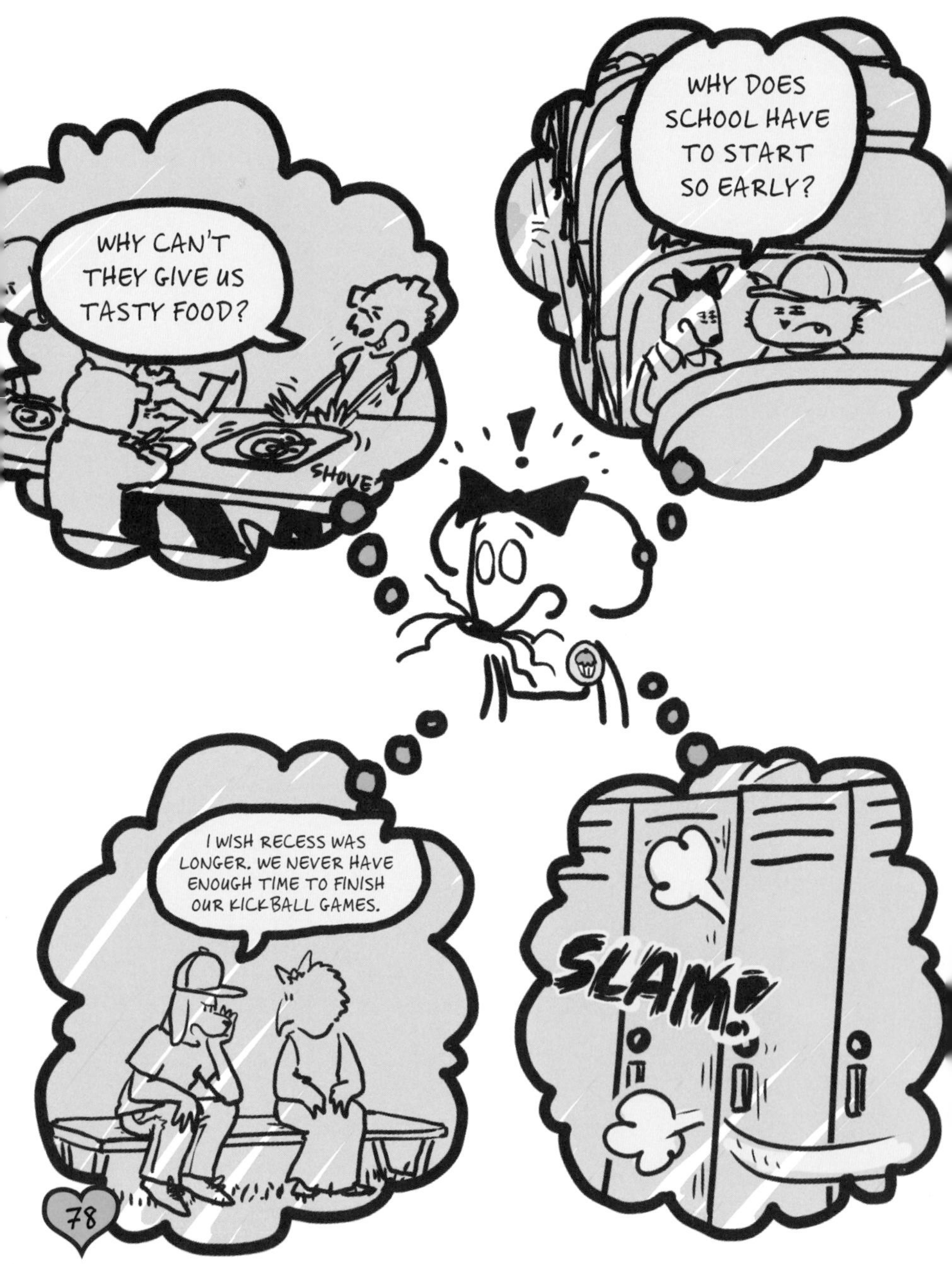
WHY CAN'T THEY GIVE US TASTY FOOD?
SHOVE
WHY DOES SCHOOL HAVE TO START SO EARLY?
I WISH RECESS WAS LONGER. WE NEVER HAVE ENOUGH TIME TO FINISH OUR KICKBALL GAMES.
SLAM!

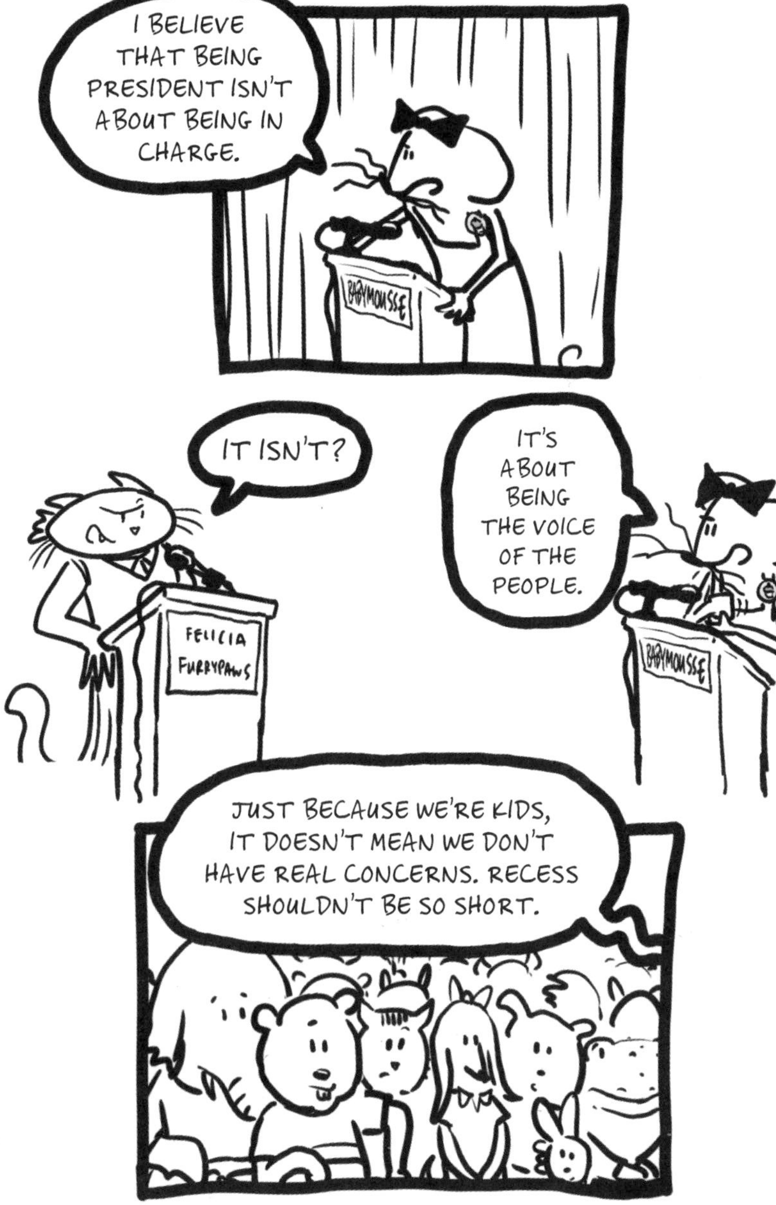
I BELIEVE THAT BEING PRESIDENT ISN'T ABOUT BEING IN CHARGE.
BABYMOUSSE
IT ISN'T?
FELICIA FURRYPAWS
IT'S ABOUT BEING THE VOICE OF THE PEOPLE.
BABYMOUSSE
JUST BECAUSE WE'RE KIDS, IT DOESN'T MEAN WE DON'T HAVE REAL CONCERNS. RECESS SHOULDN'T BE SO SHORT.

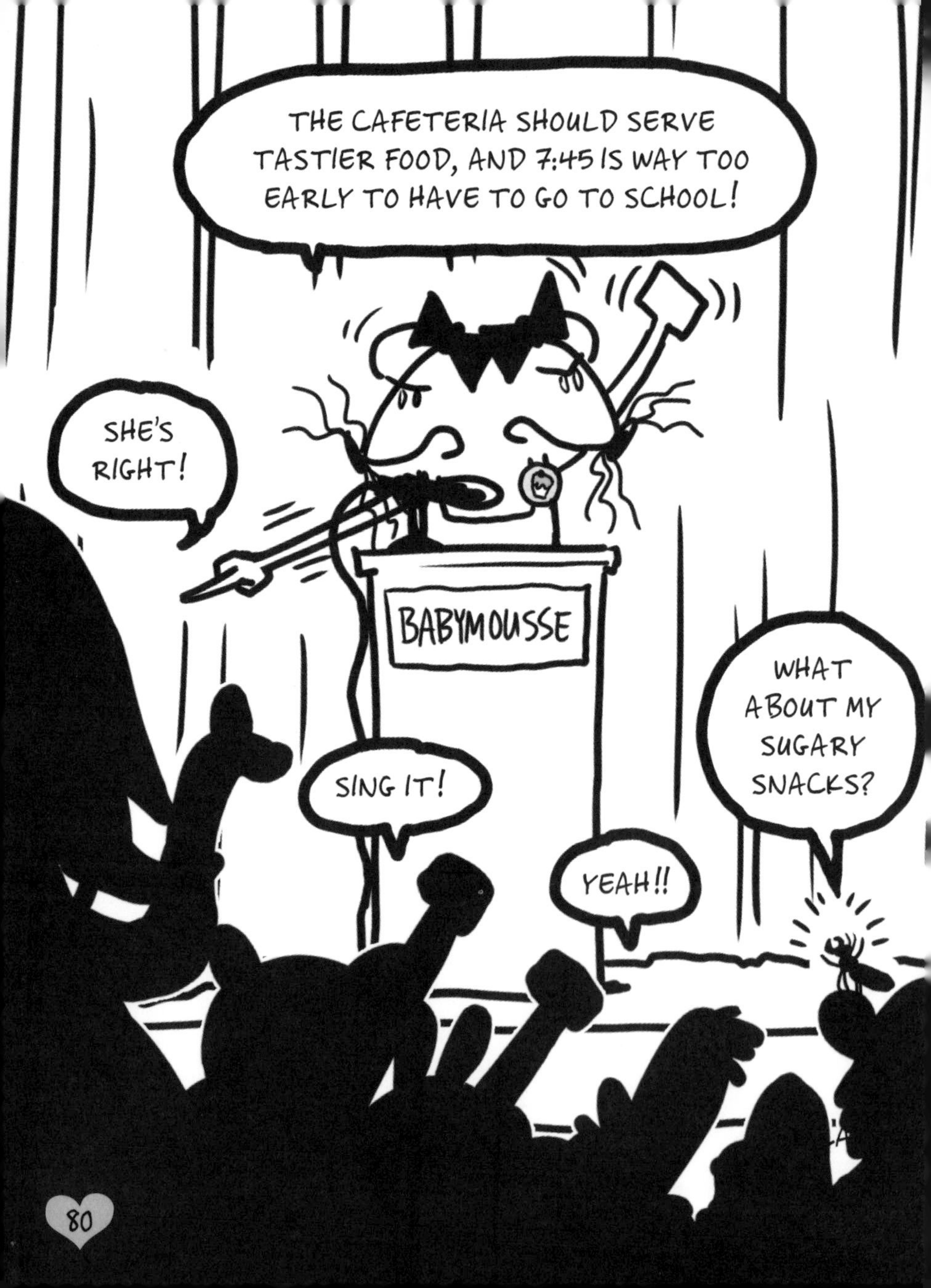
THE CAFETERIA SHOULD SERVE TASTIER FOOD, AND 7:45 IS WAY TOO EARLY TO HAVE TO GO TO SCHOOL!
SHE'S RIGHT!
BABYMOUSSE
SING IT!
WHAT ABOUT MY SUGARY SNACKS?
YEAH!!

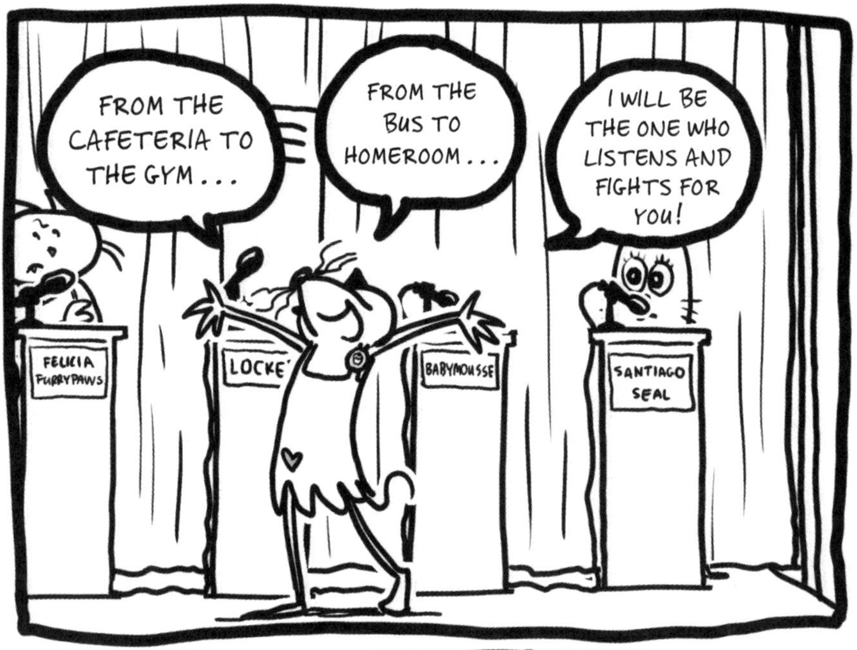
FROM THE CAFETERIA TO THE GYM . . .
FROM THE BUS TO HOMEROOM . . .
I WILL BE THE ONE WHO LISTENS AND FIGHTS FOR YOU!
FELICIA FURRYPAWS
LOCKE
BABYMOUSSE
SANTIAGO SEAL

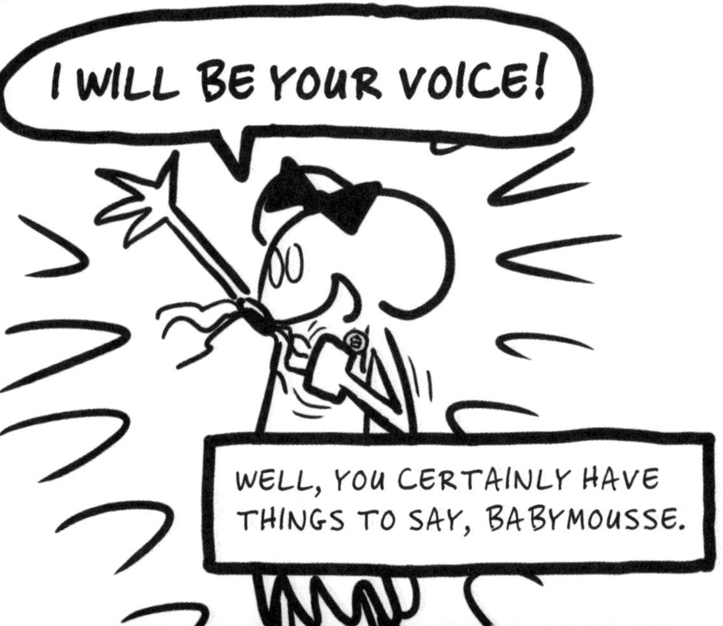
I WILL BE YOUR VOICE!
WELL, YOU CERTAINLY HAVE THINGS TO SAY, BABYMOUSSE.

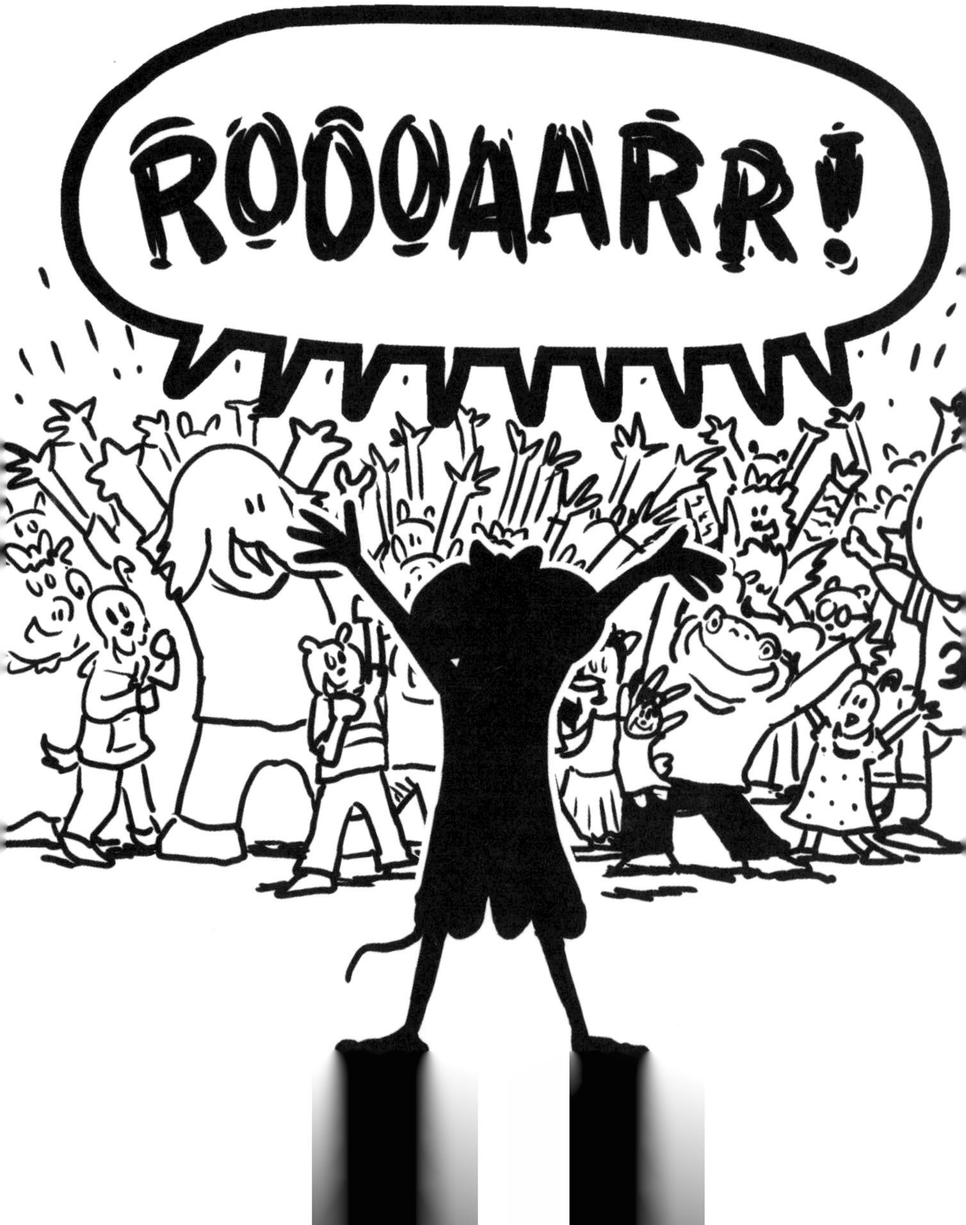
ROOOAARR!

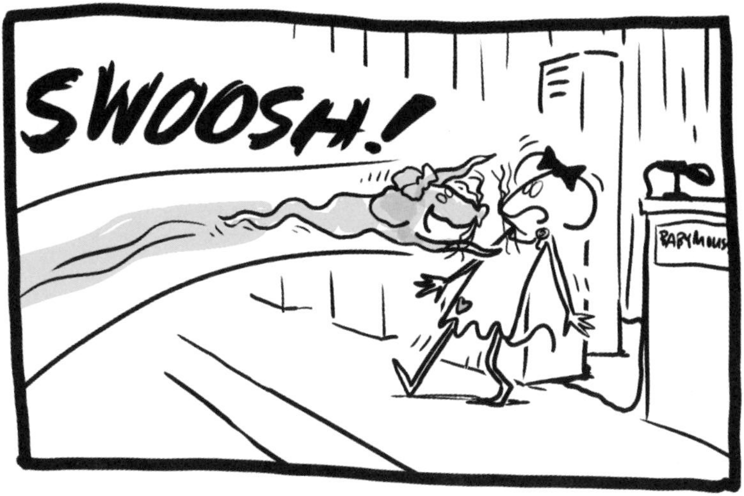
SWOOSH!
BABYMOUS

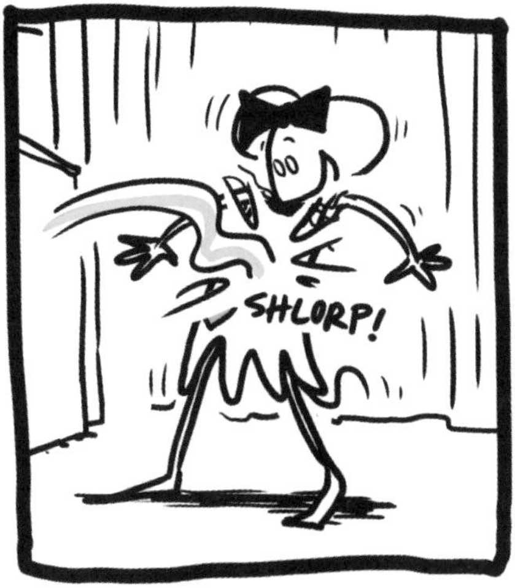
SHLORP!

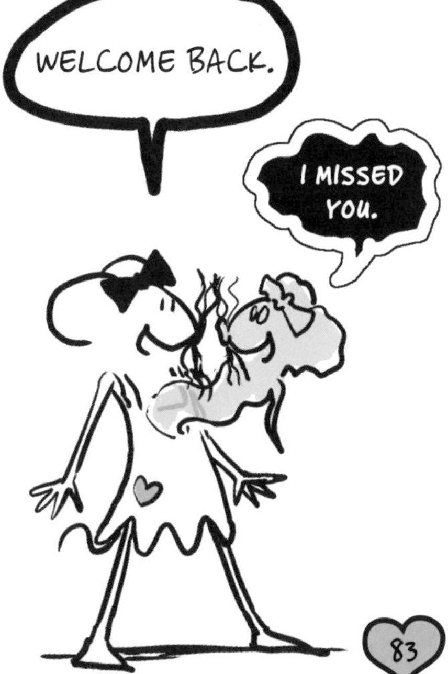
WELCOME BACK.
I MISSED YOU.

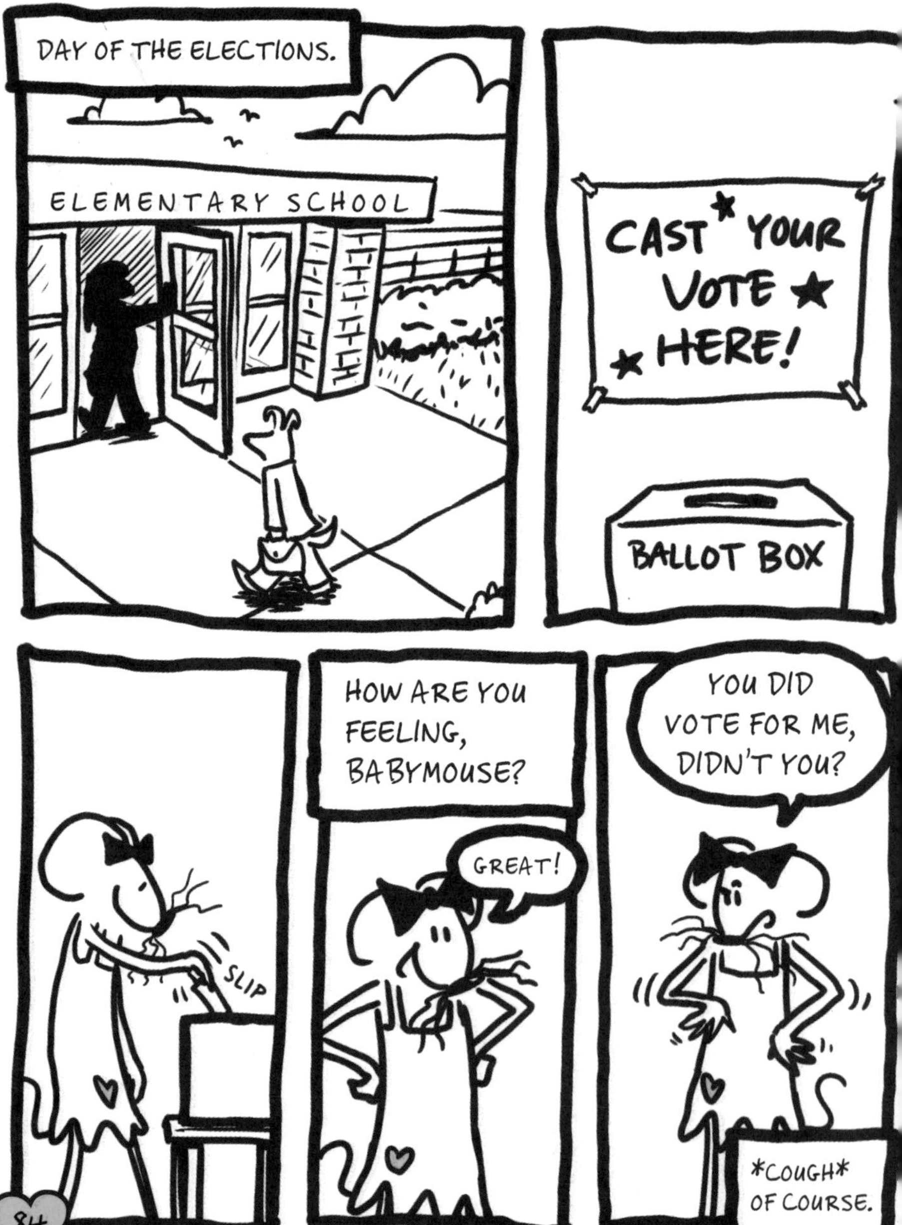
DAY OF THE ELECTIONS.
ELEMENTARY SCHOOL
CAST YOUR VOTE HERE!
BALLOT BOX
SLIP
HOW ARE YOU FEELING, BABYMOUSE?
GREAT!
YOU DID VOTE FOR ME, DIDN'T YOU?
COUGH OF COURSE.

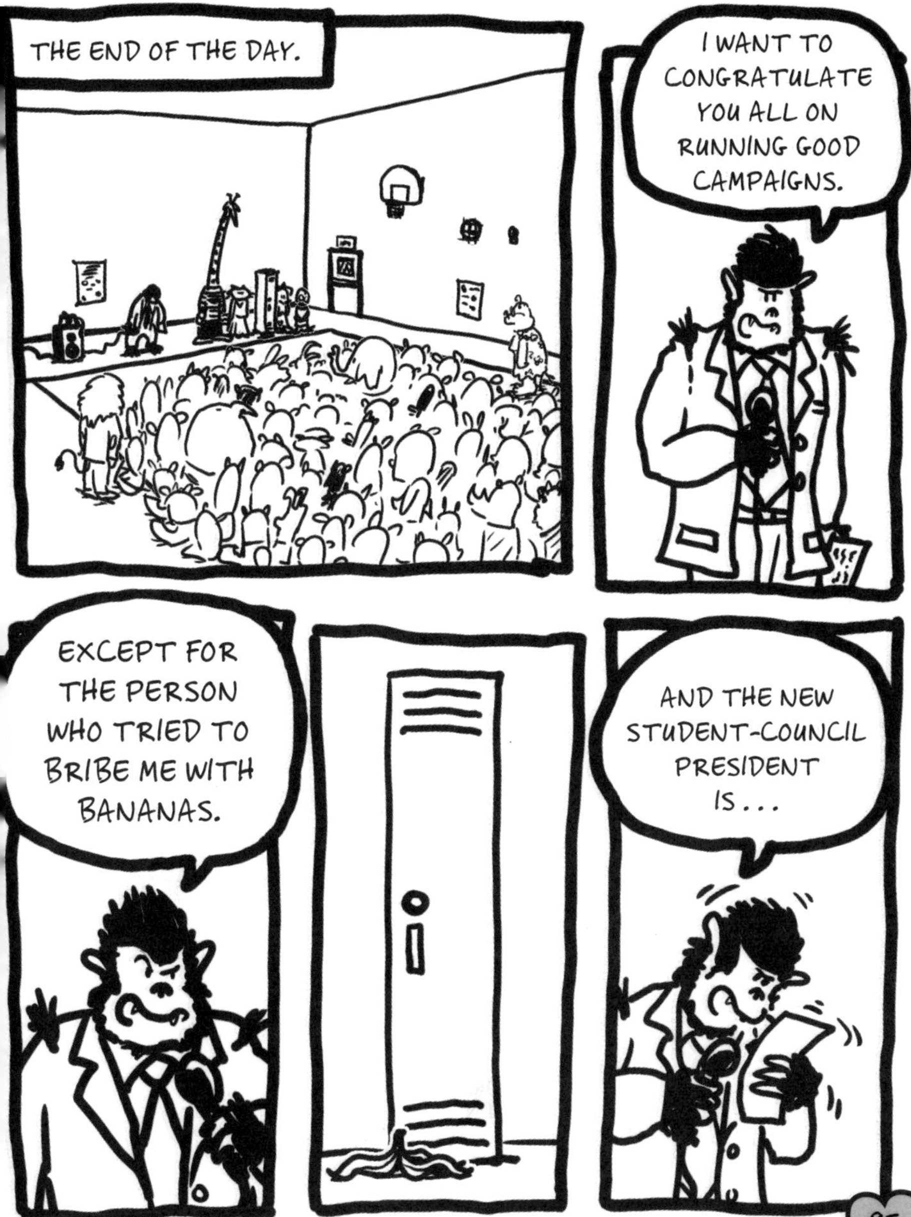
THE END OF THE DAY.
I WANT TO CONGRATULATE YOU ALL ON RUNNING GOOD CAMPAIGNS.
EXCEPT FOR THE PERSON WHO TRIED TO BRIBE ME WITH BANANAS.
AND THE NEW STUDENT-COUNCIL PRESIDENT IS . . .

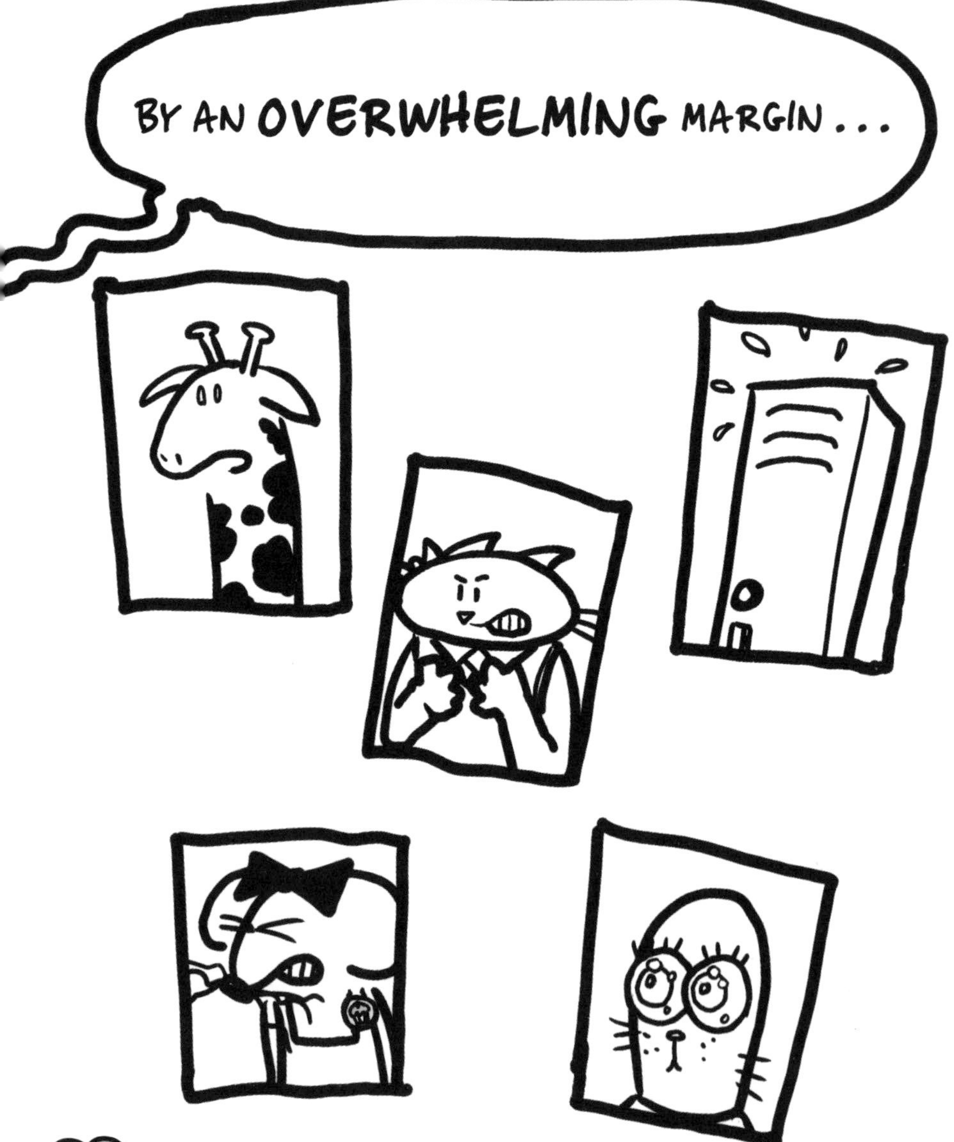
BY AN OVERWHELMING MARGIN...

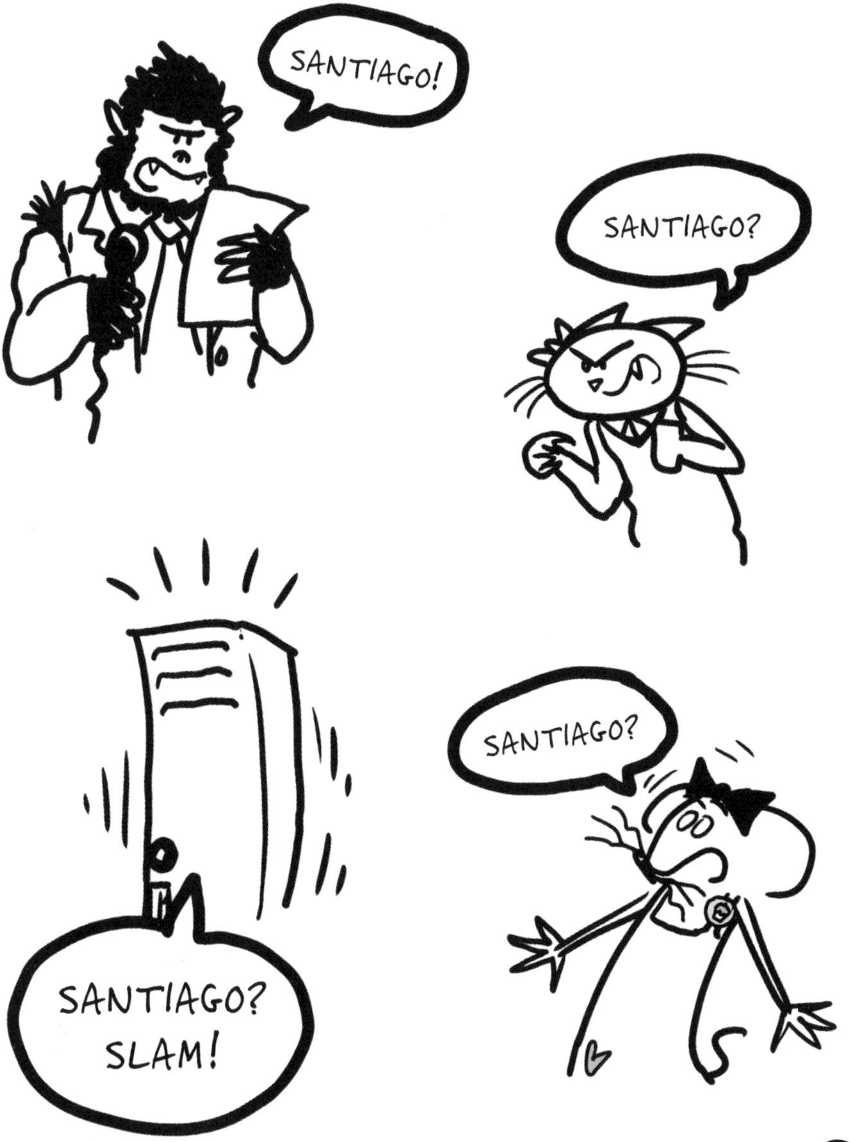
SANTIAGO!
SANTIAGO?
SANTIAGO?
SLAM!
SANTIAGO?

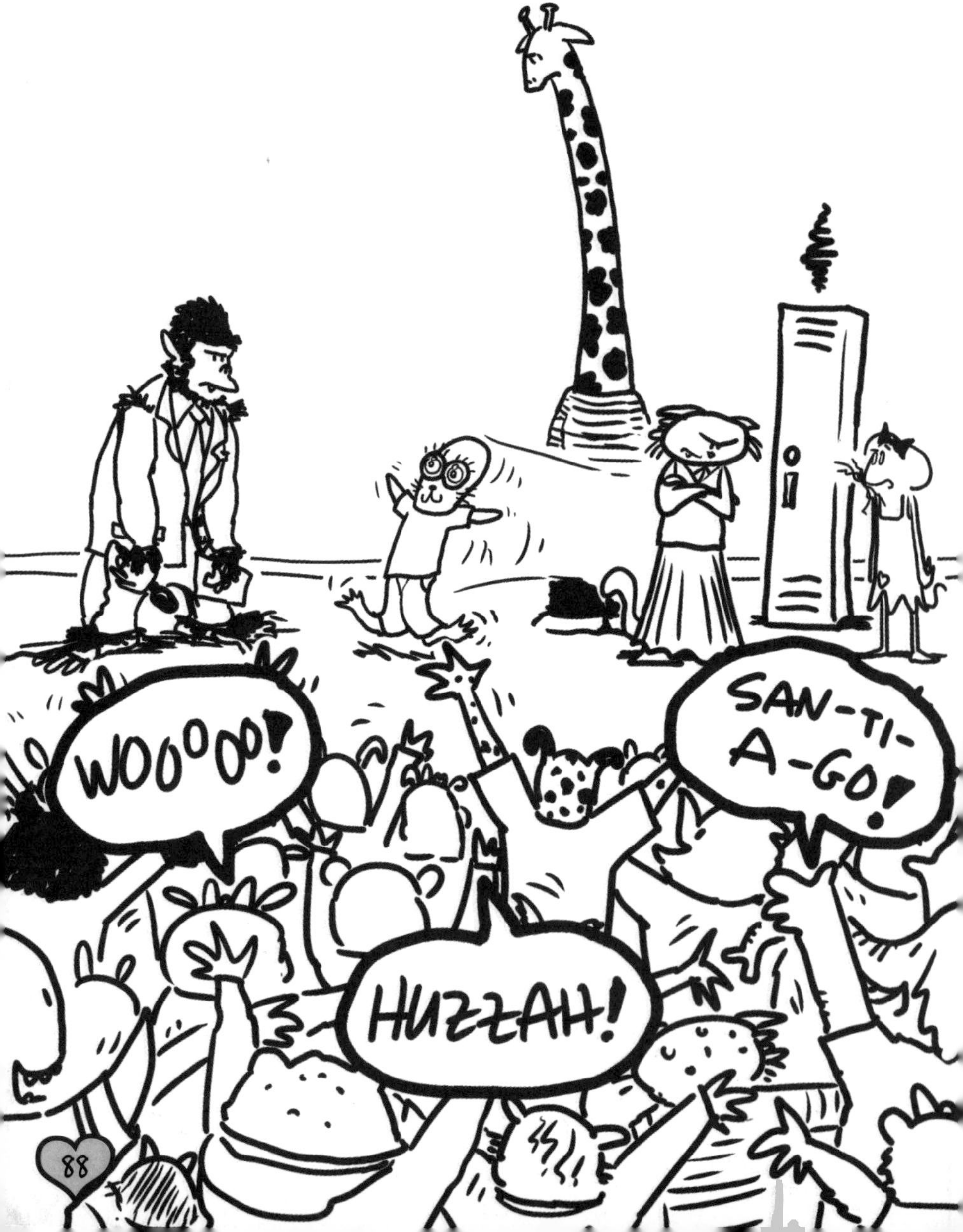
WOOOOO!
SAN-TI-A-GO!
HUZZAH!

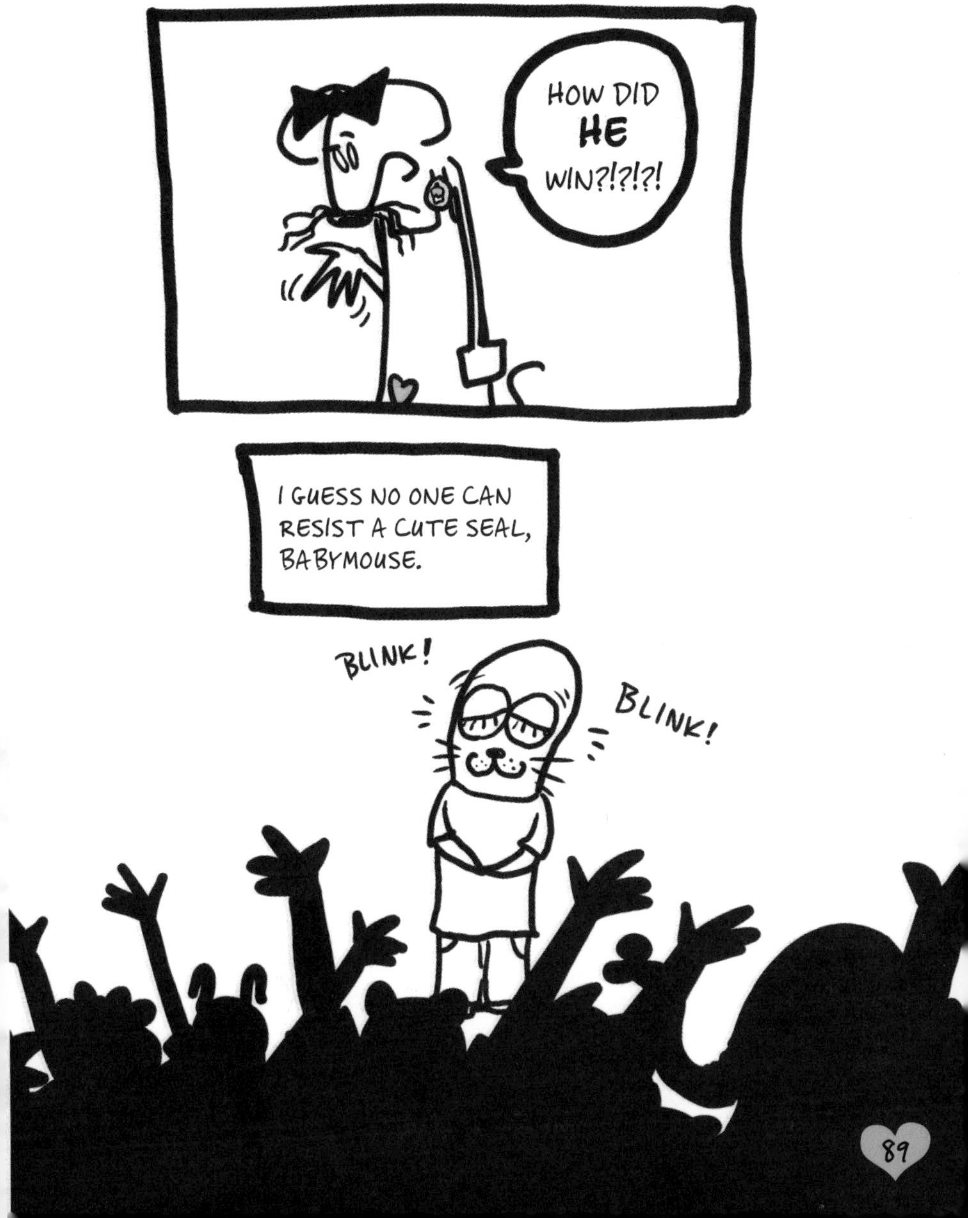
HOW DID HE WIN?!?!?!
I GUESS NO ONE CAN RESIST A CUTE SEAL, BABYMOUSE.
BLINK!
BLINK!

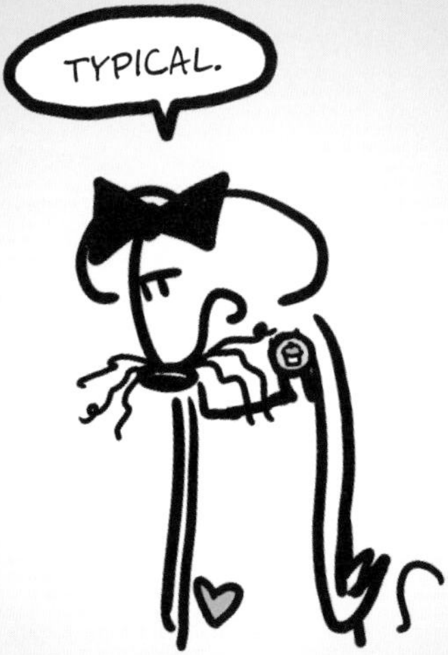
TYPICAL.

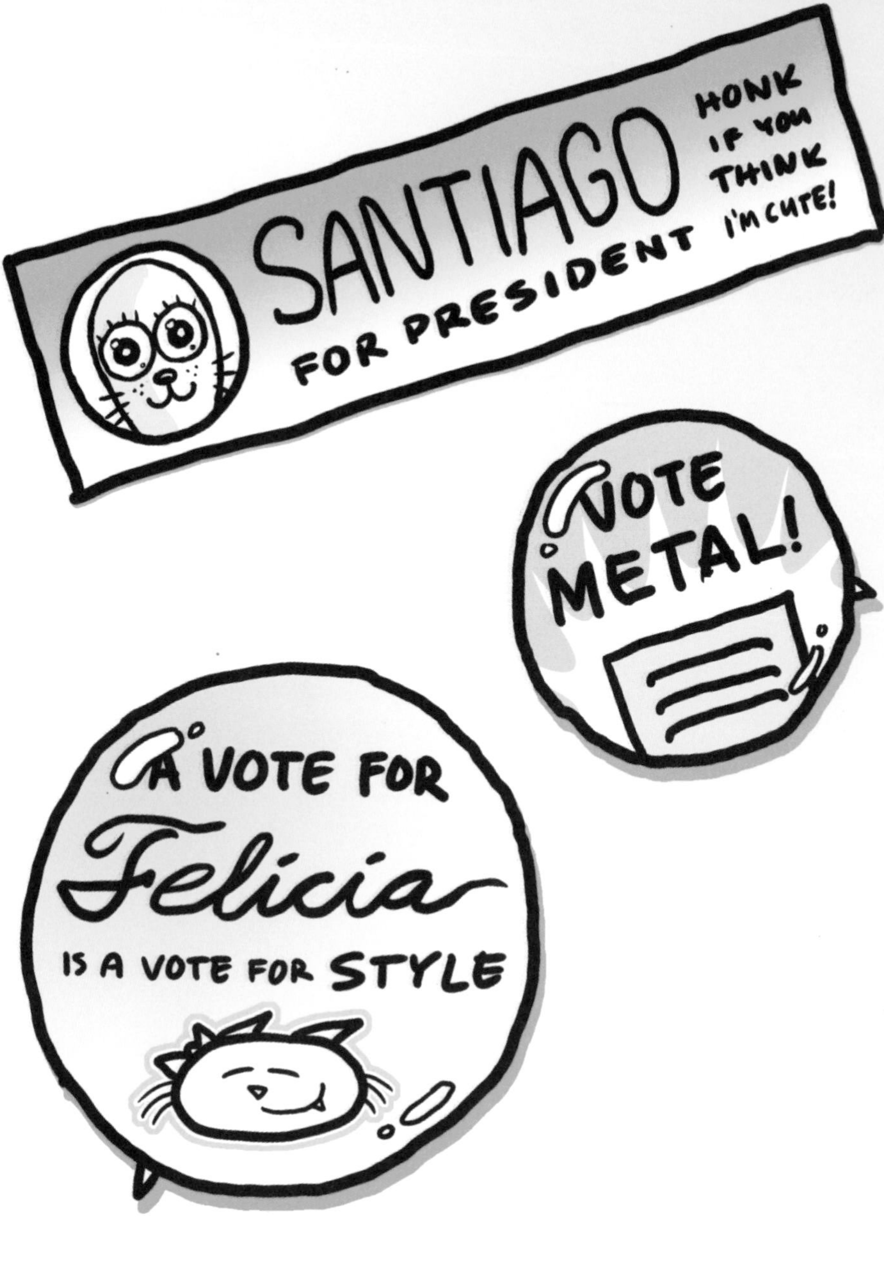
SANTIAGO
FOR PRESIDENT
HONK IF YOU THINK I'M CUTE!
VOTE METAL!
A VOTE FOR
Felicia
IS A VOTE FOR STYLE

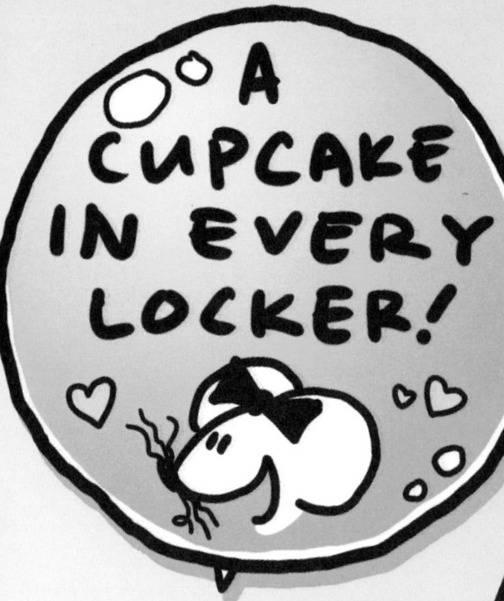
A CUPCAKE IN EVERY LOCKER!

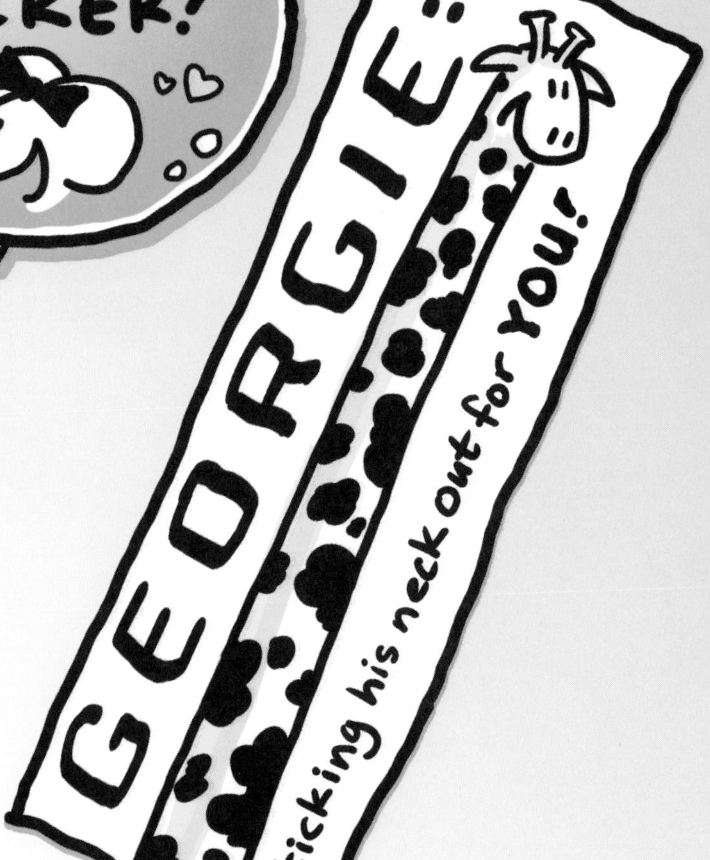
GEORGIE
Sticking his neck out for YOU!

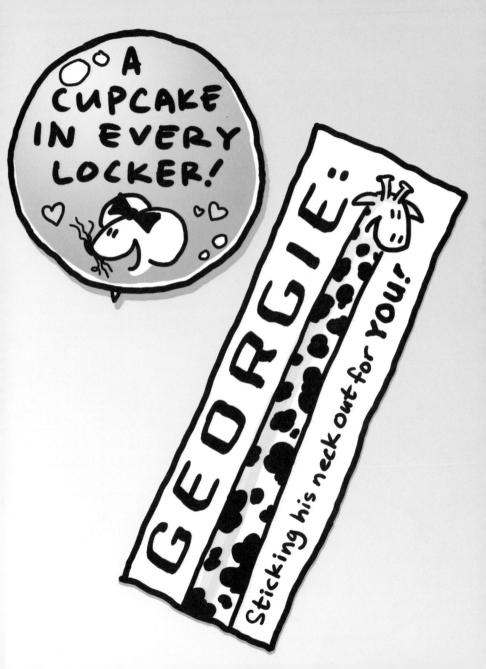

DON'T MISS THE NEXT BABYMOUSE!

EXTREME BABYMOUSE

COMING IN JANUARY 2013

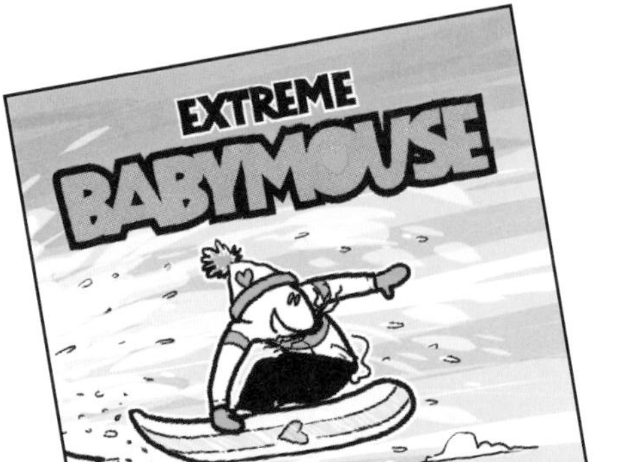
EXTREME
BABYMOUSE
JENNIFER L. HOLM & MATTHEW HOLM

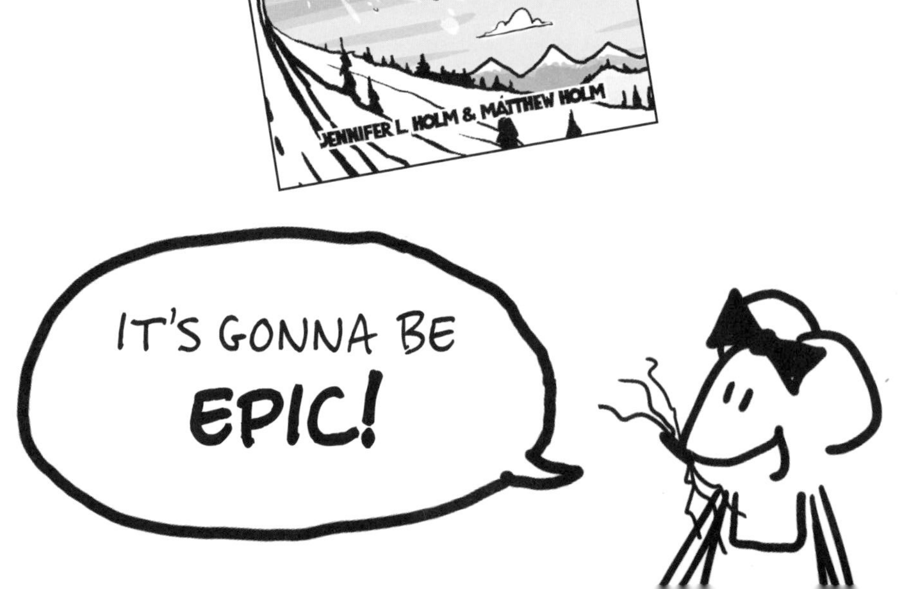
IT'S GONNA BE EPIC!

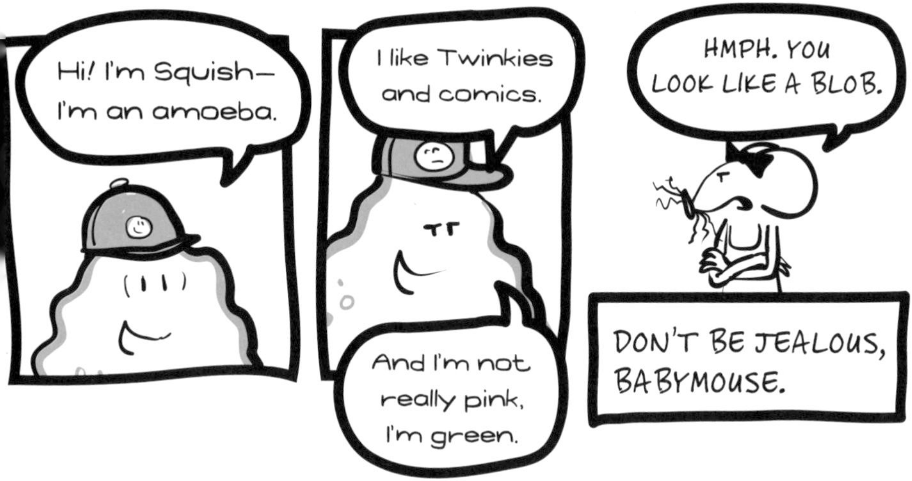
Hi! I'm Squish—
I'm an amoeba.
I like Twinkies
and comics.
And I'm not
really pink,
I'm green.
HMPH. YOU
LOOK LIKE A BLOB.
DON'T BE JEALOUS,
BABYMOUSE.

READ ABOUT
SQUISH'S AMAZING ADVENTURES IN:

#1 SQUISH: Super Amoeba

#2 SQUISH: Brave New Pond

#3 SQUISH: The Power of the Parasite

#4 SQUISH: Captain Disaster

★ "IF EVER A NEW SERIES DESERVED TO GO VIRAL, THIS ONE DOES."
—*KIRKUS REVIEWS*, STARRED

If you like Babymouse,
you'll love these other great books
by Jennifer L. Holm!

THE BOSTON JANE TRILOGY
EIGHTH GRADE IS MAKING ME SICK
MIDDLE SCHOOL IS WORSE THAN MEATLOAF
OUR ONLY MAY AMELIA
PENNY FROM HEAVEN
TURTLE IN PARADISE

THEY'RE REALLY GOOD! TRUST ME!